THE COUNT OF CHANTELEINE

A Tale of the French Revolution

PUBLICATIONS OF THE NORTH AMERICAN JULES VERNE SOCIETY

The Palik Series (edited by Brian Taves)

The Marrriage of a Marquis (*The Marriage of Mr. Anselme des Tilleuls* and *Jédédias Jamet, or The Tale of an Inheritance*)
    Contributors: Edward Baxter, Jean-Michel Margot, Walter James Miller, Kieran M. O'Driscoll, Brian Taves

Shipwrecked Family: Marooned with Uncle Robinson
    Translated by Sidney Kravitz; Introduction by Brian Taves

Mr. Chimp, and Other Plays
Translated by Frank Morlock; Introduction by Jean-Michel Margot

Around the World in 80 Days—The 1874 Play by Jules Verne and Adolphe D'Ennery
    Introduction by Philippe Burgaud; with Verne's essay "The Meridians and the Calendar," translated by Jean-Louis Trudel

Vice, Redemption, and the Distant Colony: Stories by Jules Verne and Michel Verne (Pierre-Jean, The Somber Fate of Jean Morénas, Fact-Finding Mission)
    Translated, with notes, by Kieran M. O'Driscoll

Bandits & Rebels: San Carlos and *The Siege of Rome*
    Translated by Edward Baxter; Introduction by Daniel Compère

(Other volumes in preparation)

Editorial Committee of the North American Jules Verne Society:

Henry G. Franke III	Dr. Terry Harpold
Jean-Michel Margot	Dr. Brian Taves

THE COUNT OF CHANTELEINE

A Tale of the French Revolution

by Jules Verne

Translated by Edward Baxter

Notes by Garmt de Vries-Uiterweerd

Afterword by Volker Dehs

Illustrated with the Engravings from the
Original 1864 French Publication

Edited and with an Introduction by Brian Taves
for the North American Jules Verne Society

The Palik Series

BearManor Fiction

2011

The Count of Chanteleine: A Tale of the French Revolution
by Jules Verne

For information, address:

BearManor Fiction
P. O. Box 71426
Albany, GA 31708

bearmanormedia.com

North American Jules Verne Society: najvs.org

Typesetting and layout by John Teehan

Cover design from an original 19th century French edition
Back cover sketch by Albert Robida

Published in the USA by BearManor Media

ISBN—1-59393-369-X
978-1-59393-369-2

Table of Contents

For Walter James Miller
who over four decades did so much to
advance Verne scholarship and to bring him
to modern readers

From *Famille-sans-nom* (*Family Without a Name*, 1889)

Introduction

Verne's Forgotten Swashbuckler

by Brian Taves

Topicality and history was an essential element in Jules Verne's series, the "Voyages Extraordinaires" ("Extraordinary Journeys"), and many episodes of his era were included. Six books reflected the 19th century fascination with African exploration[1] and reaching the polar regions.[2] Similarly, the Yukon gold rush that occurred late in Verne's life would be portrayed (*Le Volcan d'or* [*The Golden Volcano*, 1906]). Modern transportation, such as railroads and steamers, were found in many stories, most prominently in the chronicle of the trans-Atlantic vessel the *Great Eastern*.[3] The American Civil War became a subject, first as a contemporary event, then as history.[4] Other historical events were featured, including the Greek War of Independence, the Quebec revolt for independence, and the Sepoy revolt in India.[5]

---

1. *Cinq semaines en ballon* (*Five Weeks in a Balloon*, 1863), *Aventures de trois Russes et de trois Anglais dans l'Afrique australe* (*Adventures of Three Russians and Three Englishmen in Southern Africa*, 1872).

2. *Un Hivernage dans les glaces* (*A Winter Amid the Ice*, 1855), *Voyages et aventures du capitaine Hatteras* (*Journeys and Adventures of Captain Hatteras*, 1866), *Le Pays des fourrures* (*The Fur Country*, 1873), *Le Sphinx des glaces* (*The Sphinx of Ice*, 1897).

3. Verne told of his own voyage on the *Great Eastern* in *Une Ville flottante* (*A Floating City*, 1871).

4. *Les Forceurs de blocus* (*The Blockade Runners*, 1865), *Nord contre Sud* (*North Against South*, 1887).

5. *L'Archipel en feu* (*The Archipelago on Fire*, 1884), *Famille-sans-nom* (*Family Without a Name*, 1889), and *La Maison à vapeur* (*The Steam House*, 1880), respectively; the Sepoy revolt was also referenced in a key passage in *L'Île mystérieuse* (*The Mysterious Island*, 1874).

However, one event which must have been very close to any Frenchman's heart seems to have been treated in a very remote fashion. The French Revolution was only examined externally in *Le Chemin de France* (*The Road to France*, 1887), depicting the attack of the coalition of Austria and Prussia against the Republic. The Revolution itself, as it occurred inside France, was not part of the "Extraordinary Journeys."

Or was it?

In fact, it was meant to be included. Only decisions by Verne's primary publisher, Pierre-Jules Hetzel, and Verne's son, Michel, resulted in this absence. Verne did write a novel of the Revolution as a civil conflict, within France. And he selected a particularly vicious portion of the conflict, the suppression of a revolt near his birthplace of Nantes. *Le Comte de Chanteleine: Épisode de la Revolution* (*The Count of Chanteleine: A Tale of the French Revolution*) was serialized in three issues of the magazine *Musée des Familles* (*Family Museum*) in 1864, shortly after Hetzel's breakthrough publication of *Five Weeks in a Balloon* that won Verne best-seller status.[6] Verne's contract with Hetzel allowed the author to publish one text per year in *Musée des Familles*, since it had no affiliation with Hetzel, but soon Verne's emphasis on a new genre was becoming clear as he continued his work for Hetzel with *Voyage au centre de la Terre* (*Journey to the Center of the Earth*, 1864) and *De la Terre à la Lune* (*From the Earth to the Moon*, 1865).

Understandably, most study has dwelled on this literary genre he did so much to develop, science fiction. Nonetheless, more than half of Verne's fiction belongs to different genres, primarily adventure, along with comedy and mystery. The adventure genre formed the foundation of the "Extraordinary Journeys," and was the most often invoked formula, a staple that allowed Verne to keep up his astonishing output of one or two novels annually. During the 19th century, adventure was an emerging generic tradition, popular and saleable, and the classical forms of Sir Walter Scott and Alexandre Dumas, *père*, were adopted by Verne. This was evident in his 1850s publications for *Musée des Familles*, *Un drame au Mexique—Les premiers navires de la marine mexicaine* (*A Drama in Mexico—The First Ships of the Mexican Navy*) and *Martin Paz*. Verne's success with the genre would become notable,

---

6. For English-speaking readers, not the initial intended readership, the translation has specified the revolution of the subtitle.

especially with *Le Tour du monde en quatre-vingts jours* (*Around the World in Eighty Days*) and *Michel Strogoff* (*Michael Strogoff*), equally popular as 1870s books and when he adapted them shortly after for the stage. (Verne's theatrical version of *Around the World in Eighty Days* is also included in the Palik series.)

The Count of Chanteleine uses a form indebted to Verne's friend and idol Dumas, especially his stories of the Musketeers and Monte Cristo. The swashbuckler is an adventure type using European (or Europeanized) history as the background for heroes and villains who are largely fictional but whose conflict incarnates larger issues of government and justice. The swashbuckler adventure usually opens with oppression imposed on a peaceful land, resulting in a rebellion that calls forth a leader dedicated to the rights of the people. The swashbuckler dwells on individuals, elevating their importance amidst the background of history. With the hero's aid, either a just regime is restored or a new, improved establishment is created, replacing one that had proved liable to transgression by tyrants.

While the prototype of the swashbuckler is the myth of Robin Hood, the figure has been elaborated historically through more recent popular manifestations from the Scarlet Pimpernel to Zorro. The tenets of the genre, offering portrayals of heroes and heroines of nobility, self-sacrifice, vigor, and virtue, may be fulfilled from a variety of directions, so long as the struggle for freedom is upheld against various forms of oppression around the globe, celebrating the rise of individual freedom and self-determination. Whether the hero is a peasant rebelling against unjust rule, or a noble opposing a usurper, the motive always remains the same, to defend the broad interests of the people.

The swashbuckler offers the appeal of characters who briefly yet honorably transgress the law, yet whose ultimate impact is to uphold morality. Outlaw deeds are sanctioned, since the actual lawbreakers are those who have attempted to seize political power, often employing drastic means. Swashbucklers stress the purity of the hero's motives, never seeking personal gain, dedicated to a righteous cause and demonstrating physical and mental agility. The aristocracy in the swashbuckler is one of bearing rather than inheritance, and may encompass noble or commoner, aristocrat or peasant.

These same aspects are also evident in two earlier Verne works to appear for the first time in English in the Palik series. The bandit who provides the title of "San Carlos" is a man of low rank but born to lead, inspiring loyalty, and he and his men live for the joy of eluding the staid pursuing authorities. San Carlos and his band are entrepreneurial, selling smuggled goods, but harming no one. They are far from pirates or marauders, with no trace of blood-lust, even when a traitor comes near to exposing them. The same ethics establish the morality in *Le Siège de Rome* (*The Siege of Rome*), although this time the French army is retaking the city from Garibaldi's rebels. They are not romanticized like San Carlos, but depicted as mercenaries, obviating any sympathy for their views. There is no glory in military maneuvers for their own sake, only as the means to a restoration of the independence of the papacy, with the church temporal already in the process of a reformation. Providing fictional clarification are a trio of comrades-in-arms, attempting to foil a villain who, dismissed in disgrace from papal service, becomes a rabble-rouser, abducting an innocent woman and causing her death.

As in *The Siege of Rome*, *The Count of Chanteleine* begins by setting the historical backdrop, in a manner sympathetic to the authority of the church. An indirect result of ending special privileges for local nobility was that the state now imposed a degree of control over regions beyond what the monarchy had exerted, creating a series of administrative departments, with a determination to extinguish provincial separatism. (Piette, 88; Goodwin, 352) A Catholic and Royal "White" army assembled in March 1793, a socially-inclusive resistance that brought together all ranks, classes, and ages, men and women alike, from the entire region. (Schama, 696) Soon the Whites of the western provinces were victorious against the Blues of the revolution. The response came quickly. In the Vendée, as Verne notes in *The Count of Chanteleine*, the government "embarked on a campaign of the most horrible devastation ... pillaging, massacring, and destroying. No one, women, children, or old men, escaped their bloody reprisals." (Chapter 12) By December 23, the Catholic Royal resistance was routed, beginning a long retreat, depicted by Verne in vivid language. "Newborn children were exposed naked to all the rigors of the elements; their mothers had nothing to cover them with. Hunger and cold added their torments to all the suffering. Cattle fleeing along the same route bellowed above the sound of the storm..." (Chapter 2) Over 20,000 were involved in this long retreat, punctuated with sporadic losing battles. (Schama, 787)

Verne depicts the lack of honor on the part of the Blues, regarding their opponents as brigands worthy only of extermination, even after surrender. The Reign of Terror dehumanized adversaries as a matter of ideology, executing thousands, with some of the most notorious massacres in Nantes. (Schama, 788-789) The policy of "pacification" included routine rape and mutilation of women and children, as well as the slaughter of combatants, sometimes killed so they would fall into their own mass graves. The loss in life was at least 40,000 and quite possibly a quarter of a million or more, one third of the region's population, creating what many regard as the first modern genocide. Chapter 2 of *The Count of Chanteleine* was constructed around the results of the policies of Jean-Baptiste Carrier in Nantes, who shot hundreds of priests and executed or starved to death thousands of royalists, many of them rebellious peasants. Even Robespierre believed Carrier had gone to excess and recalled him to Paris. (Piette, 96)

The titular character of *The Count of Chanteleine* is first introduced amidst the combat, "a tall, handsome man of about forty-five. His face was bold and noble, but sad because of the powder and blood that covered it. He looked magnificent, despite his bespattered clothes. In one hand he held the pistol he had just fired and in the other his bloody and battered sword." (Chapter 1) Here Verne offers a fearless adventure hero, a man who incarnates the expected virtues of aristocracy; the fact that during the entire novel Humbert de Chanteleine is almost always referred to by his title, rather than name, indicates how his characterization was intended to embody nobility of nature emerging against a tumultuous backdrop. He is a symbol as much as he is a three-dimensional character, no less than Jean Sans-Nom stands for the rebellion against English dominion in *Family Without a Name*—and just as Jean Chouan historically gave his name to the Vendée counter-revolutionaries, the *chouans*.

Chanteleine is descended from one of the oldest lines in Brittany, whose lands have belonged to them since time immemorial, and which have always been semi-autonomous in their relation to the crown. (In this way, Chanteleine stands apart from any royal tyranny.) In fact, there had long been an unusually close relationship in Brittany between peasantry and feudal superiors. (Goodwin, 334) After the Revolution, many Breton nobles, isolated and under pressure, had renounced their seigneurial rights, accepting the new order. (Piette, 87)

The frontispiece for Verne's 1893 Dickensian novel of Irish children.

The swashbuckler formula that Verne used, of a nobly-born hero with the characteristics desired for one of his background and education, was misread by Hetzel as implying a political agenda. Evidently Hetzel failed to notice the same formula evident elsewhere in many other "Extraordinary Journeys." Michael Strogoff's trek served to uphold the rule of the Czars, situated opposite barbaric foreign invaders. The novel is not an attempt to analyze and support the Russian social order, but is a tribute to heroism—allowing the Czar and Grand Duke, as well as Michael, together with a pardoned rebel and his daughter, to overcome danger to the motherland. Dakkar is a prince leading his people in the Sepoy revolt against British colonial rule before becoming Captain Nemo of the *Nautilus*. James Burbank is a civic leader among the lesser white gentry of Florida in *North Against South*. Like Strogoff, Dakkar, and Burbank, the Count of Chanteleine stands out among many of those around him, and no less than Dakkar in India, the count was to be found in the midst of the resistance for ten months, "always in the front ranks, [taking] part in all the victories and all the defeats." (Chapter 1)

However, rather than the titular figure, the primary character in *The Count of Chanteleine* is his peasant-born friend and right arm, Kernan, through whom most of the narrative is told. No less than the count, Kernan is presented as a bold adventurer.

> The peasant was wearing a brown woolen cap with a broad brimmed hat on top, surrounded by a rosary. The hat cast a shadow over his energetic and rugged face.... On his feet he wore a pair of enormous, badly damaged clogs... A goat-skin flung over his back completed the Breton's attire. The hilt of a cutlass protruded from his belt with its large buckle, and his right hand gripped the barrel of a musket.
>
> This peasant must have been extremely powerful. Indeed, he had a reputation in his region for incredible, even superhuman, strength. Stories were told of his astonishing deeds, and the terrible wrestler had never met his match at any of the festivals in Brittany. (Chapter 2)

Kernan is a man of no exceptional birth, but serves the count and his family and is rewarded with complete trust, to the extent that the count's daughter refers to Kernan as her uncle, and he refers to her as his niece. There is no social differentiation here; Verne vitally portrays the mixing of class backgrounds. Since childhood, the count and Kernan have never been separated, giving him an unusual education for his class. The count would have preferred leaving his family and castle in Kernan's hands during his absence, but it was impossible for the two not to fight alongside one another like brothers. Kernan is the hope for France's future, a melding of the best of peasant background and noble education, just as the count represented the country's best traditions.

The hero's personal enemies in the swashbuckler are often the same as those who menace society at large. The contrast with those who have misdirected the Revolution is reflected in Kernan's mirror image, Karval, the antagonist of *The Count of Chanteleine*. Like Kernan, Karval had also been a servant of the count, but after two years he was discovered to have stolen from the household—just as Andreani betrayed the papal trust in *The Siege of Rome*. Chanteleine regarded dismissal as adequate punishment, far more lenient than the peasants would have inflicted on Karval, as one who had disgraced their class. While the Count displayed Christian forgiveness and ultimately becomes a man of God, men like Karval and Andreani take the opposite path. Andreani denounces the papacy, and Karval, expelled from the heavenly existence on the Chanteleine lands, becomes a veritable devil. He flees to Paris, which the Breton peasants regarded as an antechamber of hell, since the only one who had gone there returns a criminal.

While both Kernan and Chanteleine are noble by thought and action, Karval is craven by nature.

> Karval was a man of medium height, with the kind of face that is produced over time by hatred, pettiness, and meanness. Every new vice sank in and left its mark. He was not lacking in intelligence, but one had the impression, on seeing him, that he must be a coward. Like many heroes of the Revolution, he was blood-thirsty out of fear, but out of fear also he was inflexible and without human feeling. (Chapter 5)

He is an opportunist, fueling the savagery of the Terror in his own desire to be among its leaders. At one point, accompanied by "his bloody mob," Karval is "hideous, blood-stained, nearly drunk, driving before him the elderly, the wounded, women, children, and unfortunate

Vendéan prisoners, plucked out of the routed grand army and now on their way to the scaffold." (Chapter 6) Similarly, Andreani in *The Siege of Rome* urged Italian revolutionaries of 1849 to imitate the violence in France sixty years earlier.

Verne is at pains to portray Chanteleine as a wise, beneficent figure in his district, the opposite of the exploitative aristocrat whom Verne mentions in other passages. The Chanteleines are so beloved by their peasants, it is noted, that they could have given lessons to the kings of France. For twenty years, Madame Chanteleine "devoted herself entirely to the happiness of those who came to her. Since she knew

The Fingal Caves in *Le Rayon vert* (*The Green Ray*, 1882)

that by doing good she made her husband happy, she was continually seen at the bedside of the ill, taking in old folk, providing instruction for children, and founding schools." Her 17-year-old daughter Marie had followed her in these good deeds. (Chapter 4)

Despite the wish of the count's wife and daughter to fight alongside him, as other women of a similar station had done, the count insisted they remain at home, seemingly safe. However, once the retreat has begun, the Count must leave the fighting to save his family, who reassume primary importance in his life. This narrative device is also essential for Chanteleine and Kernan to experience the atrocities that have happened away from the front lines. Arriving home, he learns that his wife was killed by the Republicans after they seized his castle, and Marie taken prisoner. As in Verne's *Paris au XXe siècle* (*Paris in the 20th Century*), written about the same time, there is a vivid scene in a cemetery, as the count grieves for his wife and believes his daughter has also perished.

In depicting the excesses of the French Revolution by centering on persecuted innocents, *The Count of Chanteleine* resembles the recent novel *A Tale of Two Cities*, published in 1859, and translated in France in 1861. Author Charles Dickens was a lifelong favorite of Verne, to the extent that in discussing a much later Verne novel, *P'tit-Bonhomme* (*Little Boy*, 1893), an Irish social drama, he would publicly acknowledge his debt to the Englishman. However, *The Count of Chanteleine* suggests that *Little Boy* was not the first case of Verne's Dickensian inspiration. Marie is saved through a substitution and sacrifice, evocative of the climax in *A Tale of Two Cities*, when Sydney Carton gives his life so that Charles Darnay may live and marry the woman both love, Lucie Manette. The Chevalier Henry de Trégolan holds a pardon for his sister, but is only minutes too late to save her from the guillotine. "'My poor sister's head,' went on the chevalier, sobbing, 'had just rolled onto the scaffold as I watched.'" (Chapter 7) Still dazed, he realizes he has the means to save the life of another young woman, and Marie, facing death herself, is the lucky beneficiary.

Following this ordeal is a more peaceful interlude in Douarnenez, a fishing village, finding refuge with Locmaillé, a 60-year-old former Trégolan family servant. Henry, Kernan, and Chanteleine already have the experience to join Locmaillé as fishermen, demonstrating that these nobles were no idlers even before the Revolution. Following the genre's

Frontispiece for *The Road to France* (1887)

demands for an admirable aristocrat, Chanteleine and Henry have no feeling of entitlement; they are able to make their own way, ready to turn their hand to whatever may be needed, whether the sword or the skills of the working class. Marie, for her part, becomes a seamstress; she is never helpless and constantly meets the challenges of a new, post-aristocratic era. As Verne narrates, "At that time there were many upper-class émigrés who had to earn their living by working with their hands. It was not demeaning; quite the contrary." (Chapter 11) Henry and Marie begin to fall in love, fulfilling another requirement of the formula; such equally admirable individuals are well suited to one another not only by birth but just as importantly by deed. They represent the new, post-nobility couple, suited to a new social order that will place very different demands on their lives than those faced by their ancestors.

For Chanteleine, the Revolution has brought about an irrevocable change in his position, one which also gives him a new calling. Unlike Dakkar/Nemo, the count does not seek vengeance, although he has suffered almost as much. Chanteleine is constant and devout, with his motto, "For God and the King." For him as for his fellow counter-revolutionaries, the divine and the potential justice of the monarchy are intertwined.

Faith, after nobility, is the second phase of Verne's narrative in *The Count of Chanteleine*, just as it had been in *The Siege of Rome*. Nowhere did the opposition to the Civil Constitution coalesce in quite as widespread a way as in the Vendée. The Bretons had already long resented any lay interference into spiritual matters. (Goodwin, 333-334) Increasing food shortages and the confiscation of local crops for the urban centers were followed by a conscription order for 300,000 local men for the army. Counter-revolution was finally impelled by the government's systematic dismantling of the church and its authority, subverting the religious order. (Piette, 90)

Before the Revolution, the clergy had enjoyed considerable power but used it wisely, according to *The Count of Chanteleine*. No less than the aristocracy must embody heroic virtues to be justified within the story, so too the priesthood must serve both their parish and God. This, too, follows formula, since in the adventure genre, the most prized men of God combine the spiritual life with a ministry that actively includes fighting injustice—not sacrificially "rendering unto Caesar." Verne situates faith as not only central in this particular episode of French history, but as crucial to any people's needs in time of upheaval and rebellion. Chanteleine observes, "I have seen them celebrating mass on a small, isolated hill, with a wooden cross, earthenware vessels, and vestments of coarse cloth. And then I have seen them rushing into the thick of battle, crucifix in hand, helping, comforting, absolving the wounded, even in the face of Republican cannon fire. I thought they were more to be envied there than they were before, in all the pomp of religious ceremonies." (Chapter 10)

The new civil constitution forced priests to sign an oath of secular superiority over the spiritual realm. Those who refused faced prison,

Natalis, the soldier, in *The Road to France*

exile, or death. However, any priests who agreed to the oath were rejected by the church itself as well as the parishioners. In *The Count of Chanteleine*, one of the best of these was Yvenat, accepting a constitution signed by the king, but rejected by the peasants as a renegade and demon. He takes refuge on an island, where the population expects him to starve to death, and only the Christian charity of Kernan rescues him. Chanteleine regrets that the Revolution's impact has been to elicit such behavior, but he also says of Yvenat, "He didn't realize what a sublime role a priest plays during these times of upheaval and terror." (Chapter 10) Meanwhile, the Committee of Public Safety is too busy to avenge their priest.

With the churches shunned, newborns were not baptized, the dying did not receive the last rites, and marriages could not be performed. (Schama, 699) As a widower, Chanteleine is free to meet those spiritual needs by completing his youthful theological studies. He is ordained with the assistance of a bishop in hiding, as those who still practiced the true faith could only do so effectively underground. (Piette, 91) This confirms Chanteleine's own circle of nobility, transforming from beneficent landowner, to fighter, to spiritual healer. He begins to secretly minister to the people, appearing for baptisms, last rites, and other rituals, and in the most vivid scene, in a church service inside a cavern of the Morgat Caves so that his daughter may be married.

In the dramatic highlight, the fishing flotilla enters an area accessible only at high tide, eager for spiritual succor and the celebration of the wedding of Henry and Marie. Potentially, it should be the place of romance, as occurs during the rescue in the Fingal Caves of Staffa in Verne's later novel, *Le Rayon vert* (*The Green Ray*, 1882). Instead, in *The Count of Chanteleine*, love and natural beauty are inverted. A warship appears, Karval leading its boats filled with soldiers, firing indiscriminately into the congregation. The literal bloodbath in the Morgat Caves serves as another indication of the Republic's treatment of its citizens, no less horrendous than the novel's scenes of the guillotine.

Trailing Karval to try and save the count, Kernan captures his adversary at last. Offering a bribe, Karval proves to be the most cowardly of men, and Kernan replies, "God would damn me, you wretch, if I didn't kill you with my own hand." (Chapter 15) However, he does permit Karval to make his confession, a practice of the Vendée partisans toward the Republicans. When Kernan and Karval locate a priest, it is none other than Yvenat, who is as terrified as Karval and gives him a cursory absolution. Fleeing, Yvenat hears a cry, as Karval is thrown from the rocks into the bay—a natural execution, so unlike the mechanical process of the guillotine.

The swashbuckler offers the comforting myth that any tyranny, no matter how formidable the arms and forces marshaled in its support, may be defeated by civilians. Despite inferior weapons, just as important is their sense of strategy and belief in justice, combined with the magnetism and skill of a hero's leadership. Plots frequently end with the principal villain meeting his death at the hands of the hero. *The Siege of Rome* had been more exceptional in this regard; only in the defeat of the rebellion is there consolation, with the villain escaping, and a tragic outcome for the heroes.

Despite the vengeance against Karval, the danger remains; Chanteleine has been sentenced as both an aristocrat and a priest. Before Kernan can attempt a rescue, however, there is a historical reverse, as adventure becomes intertwined with the background of its story. Even as children have been enlisted to operate the guillotine to indoctrinate youth in the Republic's enemies, the public's mood has shifted. At dawn on July 27, 1794, the 9th of Thermidor, the telegraph from Paris brings news to the provinces of Robespierre's death. With the Terror having consumed its own perpetrators, there is a national sense of satiation and revulsion. Pity triumphs over anger, and divine providence allows the count and his family to escape imminent death.

So ends "this episode, taken from the darkest days of the Terror." (Chapter 16) For Chanteleine himself, his own aristocratic position is abandoned in favor of trying to fill the void to assist the people in practicing the true faith. Eventually the count returns to his parish, preferring his humble priestly duties to the higher offices offered him. Answerable only to the church, not the state, he is no longer the count, but the curé of Chanteleine. History has allowed him to achieve his apotheosis, no less than did Dickens's Sidney Carton through sacrifice.

Two books on this episode of history were in Verne's library, Adolphe Thiers's nine volume *Histoire de la Révolution française* (*History of the French Revolution*, 1834), and Louis de Carné's novel, *Un Drame sous la Terreur. Guiscriff, précédé d'une notice historique sur la Chouannerie* (*A Drama under the Terror. Guiscriff, Preceded by a Historical Note on Chouannerie*, 1835). The most prominent such work had been Honoré de Balzac's 1829 breakthrough novel, *Les Chouans* (*The Chouans*). Following the style of Walter Scott, *The Chouans* was bound to have resemblances since both derived from the same tradition, but there were just as many divergences in terms of plot and characterization.[7]

Others followed the publication of *The Count of Chanteleine*, including Émile Erckmann and Alexandre Chatrian's *Histoire d'un Paysan* (*History of a Peasant*, 1867) and Victor Hugo's last novel, *Quatre-vingt-treize* (*Ninety-Three*, 1874). These were different from Verne's approach, or that of Balzac, who depicted the trickery of the police as worse than that of the brigands. Hugo, for instance, sides with the Republic, and while his monarchists and revolutionaries are both sympathetic, the Bretons are regarded as savages.

Today, *The Count of Chanteleine* is more readily recognizable as typical of stories of the French Revolution, in which the new authorities, driven to the point of fanaticism by their zealotry, have become as cruelly power-hungry as their predecessors. The frenzy of the blood-hungry mob and the specter of the guillotine provide suspense, hinging on the danger to innocents. To rescue them requires courage, daring, and impersonation. The focus on individual aristocrats and their best traits make them sympathetic, and there are elements of the old order to be prized even while acknowledging the abuses by the upper class. Verne's theatrical collaborator Adolphe d'Ennery composed the stage play, *Les Deux Orphelines* (*The Two Orphans*, 1874), telling of two persecuted heroines, sisters, one of them blind, during the Terror. Verne's one-time patron, Dumas, extensively utilized the French Revolution as a setting, with characters sympathetic or antipathetic because of their actions, not because of their political preferences. *Le Chevalier de Maison-Rouge* was published in 1845, followed by the "Marie Antoinette" cycle that lasted for a dozen years with such novels as *Joseph Balsamo*, *Mémoires d'un médecin*,

---

7.   Balzac offered exciting episodes offering nobility, heroism, and the use of disguise on a journey in delineating the opposing historical forces of the peasants and the military. The Breton rebels are led by a marquis, and the Republican forces by a veteran who finds his own command superseded as a plot is hatched with a spy dispatched to seduce the marquis. They fall in love but there is no happy ending; no less a contrast with Verne's heartfelt romantic themes is Balzac's depiction of the clergy as self-serving. The setting is later than Verne's, in 1799. Balzac's dissatisfaction with the initial generic form caused him to abridge *The Chouans* considerably to meet the more "literary" standards necessary to include it in his "La Comédie humaine" in 1834. George Saintsbury, "Preface," in Balzac, 11-15; Bell, 58-68; Shaw, 82-97.

Natalis meeting his sister in *The Road to France*

Le Collier de la Reine, *Ange Pitou*, and *La Comtesse de Charny* through *Les Compagnons de Jehu*.[8] While initially more fictive, actual history becomes steadily more important, with the fictional characters embodying certain social ideas, from the old aristocracy to the peasantry.

A distinctly Anglo-American tradition emerged, following the Dickens example in *A Tale of Two Cities*, with England seeming to

---

8. These have often been translated in English under multiple titles, sometimes in several volumes; for instance, *Joseph Balsamo, Mémoires d'un médecin* is known as *Joseph Balsamo, Cagliostro, Madame Dubarry, The Elixir of Life*, and *The Countess de Charny* as *Andrée de Taverney*, or *The Mesmerist's Victim*.

offer safety from the whirlpool engulfing France. The same British youth who absorbed Verne in *Boys' Own* also read G.A. Henty's *In the Reign of Terror, the Adventures of a Westminster Boy* (1888). A particularly rich vein was established in 1903 in Baroness Emmuska Orczy's series on The Scarlet Pimpernel. This formula of the guillotine menacing those who were guilty only by birth, and rescued by master of disguise Percy Blakeney and his intrepid followers, was offered initially in a play, and later a series of novels. The stories have proven durability as mass-entertainment in a succession of screen versions. As recently as 1997, the Pimpernel's deeds formed the basis of a hit Broadway musical version that toured the United States and abroad. Other plays have echoed Orczy, such as *Le Chevalier au masque* (*The Masked Knight*) by Paul Armont and Jean Manoussi in 1913. Orczy's chief rival was Rafael Sabatini, especially in his novels *Scaramouche* (1921) and *Scaramouche the King Maker* (1931), which portray an illegitimate son of the aristocracy amidst the Revolution. A similarly complex view of the French Revolution also emerges in Sabatini's *The Trampling of the Lilies* (1906), *Venetian Masque* (1934), *The Lost King* (1937), and *Marquis of Carabas / Master-at-Arms* (1940). Sabatini was a Verne enthusiast in his youth who devoured his stories (Knight and Darley, 5).

Hetzel not only disliked the apparent pro-royalist sentiment in *The Count of Chanteleine*, but also the importance attached to the clergy. Hetzel overlooked the anti-royal sentiment, such as the story saying that the Committee on Public Safety "saved France when it was caught up in all the horrors of the civil war and threatened by the coalition." (Chapter 12) (In a similar way, *The Siege of Rome*, while supporting the papacy and priests, included criticism of scandalous behavior by cardinals.) Hetzel's literal reading ignored that Chanteleine, amidst the brutal suppression of a counter-revolution, reveals the same political sympathy with struggles for liberation that were evident in a number of Verne's colonial novels. Recently Hetzel's view of *The Count of Chanteleine* was expressed by Verne biographer Herbert Lottman, who called the book "a bedtime story for counterrevolutionaries, written in romantic tremolo." (Lottman, 107) Unfortunately, Hetzel and Lottman failed to fully grasp either the form or purpose of *The Count of Chanteleine*, utilizing the swashbuckler formula to spin a narrative around an important historical event. By contrast, more understanding was I.O. Evans, who noted in his preface to the Fitzroy edition of *The Flight to France* that *The Count of Chanteleine* "is upon traditional 'Reign of Terror' lines, with the usual traitor, the heroic counter-revolutionary movement and the virtuous aristocrats," although he still regarded the story as unworthy. (Evans, 3)

Hetzel refused to publish *The Count of Chanteleine* in book form. The author had intended to include it in an anthology, *Souvenirs d'enfance et de jeunesse* (*Memories of Childhood and Youth*) that evolved into the posthumous *Hier et demain* (*Yesterday and Tomorrow*, 1910). However, even then his son Michel preferred to replace a historical novel with fiction having a more fantastic and scientific element—some of which he authored using his father's byline. As a result, *The Count of Chanteleine* was not published in French in book form, since its appearance in *Musée des Familles*, until 1971 in Switzerland.

When Jules Verne tried another novel on the French Revolution, having been chastened by Hetzel, he avoided the pattern of Dickens and *A Tale of Two Cities*. Instead, Verne followed the lead of two other popular authors of the time who also published through Hetzel, Erckmann-Chatrian, and their series on the Napoleonic wars. For instance, their 1865 novel *Waterloo* (a sequel to the previous year's *Conscrit de 1813*) was told in the first person by an ordinary soldier, who had survived the recent battles, hoping to return to peace. The life of a married tradesman is instead interrupted as he must reluctantly take up arms once again, during the Hundred Days of Napoleon Bonaparte's return from exile on Elba.

A similar pattern was followed in *The Road to France*, although avoiding the disillusionment inherent in an account of the Emperor's disastrous fall. Verne's hero is a man of common birth, Natalis Delpierre, who has been able to rise to the rank of officer, but remains at heart a simple soldier. He is visiting his sister in Germany when war breaks out in 1792 and the foreign coalition begins to march on France. Verne hoped the resulting patriotic tone would appeal to readers of the *Magasin d'Éducation et de Récréation* (*Magazine of Education and Recreation*), although the novel was eventually published in *Le Temps* instead. (Lottman, 262) Composed in anticipation of the celebration of the centennial of the Revolution, *The Road to France* is pre-eminently a "safe" book, one which could not offend anyone, but appeal to all—unlike its predecessor.

The Road to France avoids the theme of oppression found in *The Count of Chanteleine*, and which had echoed in such other Verne adventure novels as *The Archipelago on Fire, North Against South, Family Without a Name, Les Frères Kip* (*The Kip Brothers*, 1902), and *L'Invasion de la mer* (*The Invasion of the Sea*, 1905). Rather, *The Road to France* becomes a celebration of nationalism, a motif distant from *The Count of Chanteleine*, and closer to the advocacy of the Quebec separatism found in *Family Without a Name* published two years later. Equally palatable in English speaking countries, *The Road to France* quickly appeared in Canada, England and the United States in 1888, with the title *The Flight to France*, suggesting a possible science fiction element to the casual book buyer.

While the American Revolution is not part of Chanteleine's background, it is for Natalis, who fought alongside such heroes as Washington (described as a physical "giant"), Anthony Wayne, and John Paul Jones, as well as Lafayette, and saw action at Yorktown. (Verne had planned to refer to some of these events in his unfinished 1847 novel, *Jédédias Jamet ou l'histoire d'une succession* [*Jédédias Jamet, or The Tale of an Inheritance*], translated for the first time in the Palik series in *The Marriage of a Marquis*.) France's role in helping Americans gain their freedom provides a perspective on the subsequent Revolutionary events that would take place in their own country. Natalis remarks that he learned the lessons necessary to survive his trek from Germany to France during the tough winters on the American prairies, just as Kernan had tracked Karval like an Indian. (Chapter 15)

Natalis traveled to see his sister, in the service of the Kellers, a German family of French origin, Protestants who fled the revocation of the Edict of Nantes in 1685. They retain the memory of their ancestral language and hope to return when there is greater religious tolerance. Germany had at one time offered the prospect of refuge, just as England had for Chanteleine's family. However, the modern Germans are unfavorably portrayed, physically and morally, in a manner to be expected by a French author after the Franco-Prussian War. The Prussian government has the Keller commercial fortune tied up in an endless lawsuit inspired by Dickens's bureaucratic "Jarndyce vs. Jarndyce" in *Bleak House* (1853), and their faithlessness is further demonstrated when the government dismisses all its debts to citizens

Natalis and Jean Keller in *The Road to France*

of French ancestry with the declaration of war. A planned marriage between young Jean Keller and a French bride, Martha, renders their political position even more tenuous, especially when he is drafted to serve in the Prussian army under a rival for Martha's hand, the gutturally-named Frantz von Grawert. Natalis must escort his sister and Jean's mother, along with members of the employer's family, including the fiancée and her father, back to safety behind the French lines.

Verne portrays a France in danger from the foreign machinations of the émigrés. They are willing to use the armies of other countries to war against their homeland as a means to regain their power, a view far different from the domestic focus of *The Count of Chanteleine*. Grawert's abuse compels Jean to desert, and he and Natalis are captured, and are facing a Prussian firing squad when French troops overrun their position. The timely intervention parallels the climax of *The Count of Chanteleine*, when the 9th of Thermidor preserves Chanteleine from the guillotine. *The Road to France* and *The Count of Chanteleine* both cast a decidedly proletarian figure at the center, since the latter is as much the story of Kernan. In *The Road to France*, however, there is not only no necessary opposition between aristocrat and peasant, but the divide between White and Blue is absent, and religion is only a minor element. Both books involve the return home—in *The Road to France*, to regain the safety of their homeland, but in *The Count of Chanteleine* to find the safety and peace of pre-Revolutionary France. For the Delpierres and Kellers, as for Chanteleine and his daughter, the life they knew is gone.

The Count of Chanteleine and *The Road to France* are contradictory in their tone, the latter concentrating upon the typical "Extraordinary Journey", through the border country. *The Count of Chanteleine* emphasized history, with only incidental geography. *The Count of Chanteleine*, at 30,000 words, is also about half the length of *The Road to France*, and faster paced, resembling a traditional swashbuckler. *The Road to France* is more formal and distant in its use of the adventure formula as well as in its approach to tempo; where *The Count of Chanteleine* is vibrant and dashing, *The Road to France* plods. *The Count of Chanteleine*, while a less mature work, is much higher in entertainment value. The story demonstrates a young writer able to skillfully exploit formula, while *The Road to France* reveals one compelled to follow editorial guidance. Readers of Hungarian, Italian, Russian, and Spanish have long been able to enjoy the novel, and offering *The Count of Chanteleine* in English fulfills the hope of its writer that audiences would have the opportunity to read and enjoy it.

Works consulted:

Balzac, Honoré de. *The Chouans*. Tr. Ellen Marriage. New York: Macmillan, 1901.

Bell, David F. *Real Time: Accelerating Narrative from Balzac to Zola.* Champaign, IL: University of Illinois Press, 2003.

Compère, Daniel. "À la recherche des systèmes nouveaux." *Bulletin de la Société Jules Verne*, No. 63 (1982): 250-258.

Courville, Luce. "Préface." In Jules Verne. *Le Comte de Chanteleine.* Nantes: Editions joca seria, 1994. Pp. 7-9.

Evans, I.O., ed. *The Fitzroy Edition of Jules Verne: The Flight to France.* London: Arco, 1966.

Gaillou, Patrick and Michael Jones. *The Bretons.* Oxford: Blackwell, 1991.

Goodwin, A. "Counter-Revolution in Brittany." *Bulletin of the John Rylands Library Manchester*, 39 (March 1957), 3226-355.

Knight, Jesse and Stephen Darley. *The Last of the Great Swashbucklers—A Bio-Bibliography of Rafael Sabatini.* New Castle, Delaware: Oak Knoll Press, 2010.

Lacassin, Francis. "Préface." In Jules Verne. *Histoires inattendues.* Paris: Union Générale d'Éditions, 1982. Pp. 7-14.

Lottman, Herbert R. *Jules Verne: An Exploratory Biography.* New York: St. Martin's, 1996.

Martin, Charles-Noël. "Préface." In Jules Verne. *L'Étonnante aventure de la mission Barsac, Œuvres romancées complètes*, vol. 49. Lausanne, Éditions Rencontre, 1971. Pp. xiii-xv.

Piette, Gwenno. *A Concise History of Brittany.* Cardiff: University of Wales Press, 2008.

Sainlot, Claudine. "Les Tribulations du Comte de Chanteleine." In Jules Verne. *Le Comte de Chanteleine.* Nantes: Editions joca seria, 1994. Pp. 121-127.

Schama, Simon. *Citizens*. New York: Alfred A. Knopf, 1989.

Shaw, Harry E. *Forms of Historical Fiction: Sir Walter Scott and His Successors*. Ithaca, NY: Cornell University Press, 1983.

Taves, Brian. *The Romance of Adventure: The Genre of Historical Adventure Movies*. Jackson: University of Mississippi Press, 1993.

Wolcott, Norman, ed. *Jules Verne's The Blockade Runners—Dual Language Edition*. St. Michael's, MD: Choptank Press, 2007.

THE COUNT OF CHANTELEINE

A Tale of the French Revolution

Chapter I

TEN MONTHS OF HEROIC WAR

On February 24, 1793 the National Convention ordered an additional levy of three hundred thousand men to fight off the foreign coalition. On March 10 of the same year, the selection of conscripts was to take place by lot at Saint-Florent, in Anjou, for that commune's contingent.

Neither the outlawing of the nobility nor the death of Louis XVI had succeeded in arousing the peasants of western France, but the dispersion of their priests, the desecration of their churches, the appointment to their parishes of curés who had taken the oath of loyalty to the Republic, and this final measure of conscription, pushed them to the limit.

"If we have to die," they exclaimed, "let's die at home."

They attacked the Convention's commissioners and, armed with their sticks, routed the militia assembled to protect the draw for conscripts.

That day marked the beginning of the war in the Vendée. The nucleus of the Catholic and Royal Army came together under the direction of the carter Cathelineau and the gamekeeper Stofflet.

On March 14 the little band captured the castle of Jallais, defended by the soldiers of the 84th and the national guard of Charonne. It was there that the Catholic Army captured its first cannon from the Republicans and baptized it *The Missionary*.

"We must produce a sequel to this," said Cathelineau to his comrades.

That sequel was the war waged by the peasants, who defeated the best troops of the Republic.

After seizing the castle of Jallais, the two Vendéan leaders captured Chollet and made cartridges from the powder meant for the Republican cannons. The movement then spread to the provinces of Poitou and Anjou. At the end of March Chantonnay was sacked and Saint-Fulgent taken. Easter was approaching and the peasants went their separate ways to perform their religious duties, to bake bread, and to replace their shoes, which had been worn out pursuing the Blues.

In April the insurrection broke out again. The men from the Marais and the Bocage assembled under the orders of Messrs. Charette, Bonchamps, d'Elbée, La Rochejaquelein, Lescure, and Marigny. Gentlemen from Brittany came to join the movement, and one of the bravest and best among them was Count Humbert de Chanteleine. He left his castle and joined the Catholic Army, then about a hundred thousand strong.

For ten months the Count of Chanteleine, always in the front ranks, took part in all the victories and all the defeats. He was victorious at Fontenay, Thouars, Saumur, and Bressuire, but was defeated at the siege of Nantes, where Commander-in-chief Cathelineau fell.

Soon all the western provinces were in revolt.

The Whites now marched on from victory to victory. Neither Aubert Dubayet, nor Kléber with his terrible Mayençais, nor the troops of General Canclaux could stand up to their indomitable zeal.

The terrified Convention ordered the land of the Vendée to be destroyed and its population driven out. General Santerre called for mines to blow up the country, and sleep-inducing smoke to smother it. He wanted to proceed by widespread asphyxiation. The Mayençais were ordered to "create a desert," as decreed by the Committee of Public Safety.

This news enraged the Royal troops. The Count of Chanteleine commanded a corps of five thousand men at the time. He fought heroically at Doué, Ponts-de-Cé, Torfou, and Montaigu, but at last the hour of defeat struck.

On October 9 de Lescure was defeated at Châtillon. On October 15 the Vendéans were driven out of Chollet, and a few days later, Bonchamps and d'Elbée were fatally wounded. Marigny and Chanteleine fought with prodigious bravery, but the Republican columns were pressing them hard. They had to think of a way of getting back across the Loire with a retreating army that still numbered forty thousand men fit for combat.

There was great confusion during the crossing. Chanteleine and his men joined the army of La Rochejaquelein, who had just been appointed commander-in-chief, and there, despite Kléber, the Whites won a great victory at Laval, the last victory of that heroic campaign.

But in fact, the Whites were disorganized. Chanteleine worked his hardest to rebuild the Royal Army, but he had neither the time nor the means. Marceau had just been appointed supreme commander by the Committee of Public Safety, and he was pursuing the Royalists with the utmost vigor. Le Rochejaquelein, Marigny, and Chanteleine had

to retreat to Le Mans and then withdraw into Laval, from which they were driven for a third time. They finally had to make their escape towards Ancenis, in order to cross back to the left bank of the Loire.

But there was no bridge and no boat. The desperate mass of peasants came down the right bank of the river and, being unable to get back to the Vendée, the fleeing multitude had no alternative but to make for Brittany. At Blain, they won a final rear-guard engagement and rushed on towards Savenay.

The Count of Chanteleine had not failed in his duty for a moment. On December 22 he and Marigny, followed by a terrified crowd, arrived at the city. With a handful of Vendéans, they lay in ambush in two small groves covering Savenay.

"This is where we must die," said Chanteleine.

A few hours later, Kléber and the Republican advance guard made their appearance. The general dispatched three companies to attack Marigny and Chanteleine's men, and, despite their stubborn resistance, flushed them out and forced them back into the city. Then he stopped and advanced no farther. Marceau and Westermann urged him to attack, but Kléber, wanting to give the entire Royal Army time to concentrate in Savenay, did not budge. He stationed his troops in the form of a crescent on the nearby heights and waited patiently for the moment to crush the Whites with a single blow.

The following night was sinister and silent. There was a feeling that the war was coming to an end. The Royalist leaders met for a high-level conference. They had nothing left to go on but the energy of despair. They could hope for no quarter, nor could they attempt to surrender, and flight was impossible. There was nothing for it but to fight and, in order to fight their best, to attack.

The next day, December 23, or, to use the language of the Republican calendar, the 3rd of Nivôse, Year II, at eight o'clock in the morning, the Whites launched their attack against the Blues.

The weather was frightful. A cold, icy rain was falling in torrents. The marshes were lost in fog and the Loire was disappearing in the mist. They would join battle in the mud.

Despite their inferior numbers, the men from the Vendée attacked with irresistible vehemence. Shouts of *Vive le roi!* were answered with shouts of *Vive la République!* The shock was terrible. The Republican vanguard buckled. Disorder set in among the front ranks of the Blues, who withdrew to Kléber's headquarters. They were running out of ammunition.

"We have no more cartridges," some soldiers shouted to their general.

"All right, then, lads," Kléber replied, "use the butts of your muskets."

At the same time, he dispatched a battalion of the 31st. Both horses and ammunition were in short supply, but the Republican general, using his headquarters staff as cavalry, threw his officers against the enemy.

The Whites were now beginning to give way. They had to go back into Savenay under hot pursuit. Their prodigious acts of bravery were in vain. They had to yield to superior numbers. Piron and Lyrot were killed with their weapons in their hands. Fleuriot, after a vain attempt to rally his scattered bands, had to break through the Republican army with a handful of men and make a dash for the neighboring forests.

Meanwhile, Marigny and Chanteleine were struggling desperately, but the ranks of the peasants were growing thinner. Death and flight were taking their toll.

"All is lost!" said Marigny to the Count of Chanteleine, who was fighting heroically beside him.

The count was a tall, handsome man of about forty-five. His face was bold and noble, but sad because of the powder and blood that covered it. He looked magnificent, despite his bespattered clothes. In one hand he held the pistol he had just fired and in the other his bloody and battered sword. He had just rejoined Marigny after breaking through the Republican ranks.

"We have no way of defending ourselves," said Marigny.

"No! No!" replied the count with a gesture of despair. "But what about those women and children and old men crowded into the city? Are we going to abandon them?"

"Never, Chanteleine! But where shall we send them?"

"On the road to Guérande."

"Go ahead, then. Take them along with you."

"But what about you?"

"Me? I'll protect you all with the last salvoes of my cannons."

"Good-bye, Marigny."

"Good-bye, Chanteleine."

The two officers shook hands. Chanteleine hurried into the city, and soon a long column of fugitives left Savenay under his orders, on the way down to Guérande.

"Follow me, lads!" cried Marigny, as he and his companion in arms parted company.

At the sound of his voice, the peasants rallied around their leader, dragging along with them two eight-pound cannons. Marigny stationed them on a height of land, in such a way as to cover the retreat. Two thousand men, the last survivors of his army, surrounded him, prepared to be cut down.

But they could not hold out against the mass of Republicans. After two hours of intense struggle, the last of the Whites, their ranks decimated, had to scatter, and fled away across the countryside.

On that day, December 23, 1793, the great Catholic and Royal Army ceased to exist.

Chapter II

The Road to Guérande

An immense crowd of terrified and desperate people was fleeing towards Guérande. They swarmed down the city's slopes in a torrent, bumping into each other at street corners, and climbed back up over the embankment. More than one, wounded during the battle by the swords of the Blues, died there. The confusion was indescribable.

In less than an hour, however, the city was completely evacuated. Marigny's resistance had given the fugitives time to collect their women, old men, and children, and push them along the way. Over their heads they could hear the cannon protecting their retreat, but when the noise stopped, the Whites greeted the silence with cries of despair. The enemy's entire army would be hot on their heels. Soon gunshots rang out, more numerous and closer, on the flanks of the long column, and many unfortunates fell, never to rise again.

The spectacle of that frantic retreat is impossible to describe. The rain fell harder than ever in the midst of a fog lit up here and there by gunfire. The road was cut off by great pools of blood-stained water, which had to be crossed at all costs. The only hope of safety lay ahead. On the right lay the vast marshes; on the left, the swollen river was overflowing its banks. It was impossible to veer away from a straight line, and any desperate Royalist who headed towards the Loire would have found its banks still littered with the corpses of Carrier's victims.

The Republican generals were harassing the fugitives, decimating or dispersing them. The wounded, the elderly, and the women were

slowing the advance of the mournful procession. Newborn children were exposed naked to all the rigors of the elements; their mothers had nothing with which to cover them. Hunger and cold added their torments to all the suffering. Cattle fleeing along the same route bellowed above the sound of the storm, and often, overcome by insurmountable fear, lowered their heads and charged through groups of people, opening bloody gaps in the crowd with their horns.

In the midst of that congestion there was total confusion of ranks, classes, and everything. Many young women from the noblest families of the Vendée, Anjou, Poitou, and Brittany, who had followed their brothers, fathers, or husbands during the great war, shared the suffering of the humblest peasant women. Some of those valiant young women, with unfailing courage, protected the flanks of the column. They could often be heard shouting, "Fire, women of the Vendée!"

Then, like the Whites, they would disperse into the thickets along the route and exchange shots with the Republican soldiers.

But night was falling. The Count of Chanteleine, with no thought for himself, was encouraging the less fortunate ones, lifting up those who were caught in the mud and others whose strength was failing them. He wondered whether the darkness would protect the refugees or enable their enemies to finish them off. His heart bled at the sight of so much suffering, and tears came to his eyes, which could not get used to the grim spectacle.

He had seen many such sights, however, during the ten-month war. At the first uprising in Saint-Florent, he had left behind his castle, his wife, his daughter, everything that he loved, and rushed to the defense of the altar. Bold, devoted, heroic, the first in the line of fire at all the battles of the Royal Army, he was one of those people of whom General Beaupuy said, "Troops who have defeated such Frenchmen as these may boast that they can defeat all the nations of Europe united against a single one."

His work was not done, however, with the defeat at Savenay. He stayed at the end of the long column, urging on the ranks of the fugitives, using his last cartridges and his saber to repel the Blues who were coming too close. But in spite of everything, he saw his comrades gradually falling behind and heard their cries as they were slaughtered in the darkness.

Then, with outstretched arms, he pushed the crowd along the road to Guérande, urging them along, hurrying them with his words.

"Move along now," he said to the laggards.

"Sir," replied one of them, "I can't do anything more."

"I'm dying," cried another.

"Help me! Help me!" said a woman beside him, who had just been hit by an enemy bullet.

"My daughter! My daughter!" cried a mother who had been suddenly separated from her child.

The Count of Chanteleine went from one to another, consoling, supporting, and helping, but he felt overwhelmed.

About four o'clock in the afternoon a peasant came up to him. Despite the darkness and the fog, he recognized the man.

"Kernan!" he exclaimed.

"Yes, my lord."

"And alive!"

"Yes, but let's keep going, let's keep going," replied the peasant, trying to pull the count along.

"And what about these poor people?" he said, indicating the scattered groups. "We can't just leave them."

"Your courage will accomplish nothing, my lord. Come! Come!"

"Kernan, what do you want of me?"

"I want to tell you that great misfortunes are in store for you."

"For me?"

"Yes, my lord. Madame the Countess, my niece Marie…"

"My wife! My daughter!" cried the count, gripping Kernan's arm.

"Yes. I've seen Karval!"

"Karval!" exclaimed the count, drawing the other man out of the crowd.

The peasant was wearing a brown woolen cap with a broad-brimmed hat on top, surrounded by a rosary. The hat cast a shadow over his energetic and rugged face. His long, blood-stained hair fell down over his broad shoulders. Cloth breeches covered his legs in loose folds down to his bare knees, which were red with the cold, and the lower part of his legs was wrapped in gaiters, held in place by colorful garters. On his feet he wore a pair of enormous, badly-damaged clogs, and he was standing on a patch of blood-soaked straw. A goat-skin flung over his back completed the Breton's attire. The hilt of a cutlass protruded from his belt with its large buckle, and his right hand gripped the barrel of a musket.

This peasant must have been extremely powerful. Indeed, he had a reputation in his region for incredible, even superhuman, strength. Stories were told of his astonishing deeds, and the terrible wrestler had never met his match at any of the festivals in Brittany.

His torn, stained, and bloody clothing bore eloquent witness to the role he had played in the Catholic Army's final battles.

He followed the Count of Chanteleine with long strides. The count, in order to make better time, went along the ditches, which were half-full of water and mud. Kernan's words had terrified him. When he reached the head of the column he found himself near a little wood, a sort of thicket, into which he pushed the Breton.

"You saw Karval?" he asked, his voice breaking.

"Yes, my lord."

"When?"

"During the fighting. Amongst the Blues."

"Did he recognize you?"

"Yes."

"And did he speak to you?"

"Yes, after he fired his pistols at me."

"You're not wounded, are you?" asked the count quickly.

"No, not yet," replied the Breton with a sad smile.

"And what did the scoundrel say to you?"

"He said, 'We'll be waiting for you at Chanteleine Castle,' and then he disappeared into the smoke. I tried to catch up with him, but I couldn't."

The count repeated the words, "We'll be waiting for you at Chanteleine Castle. What did he mean by that?"

"Nothing good, my lord!"

"And what was he doing in the Republican army?"

"He was in command of a troop of criminals like himself."

"Ah! A worthy officer of the armies of the Convention! I drove him out of my home for stealing."

"Yes, the villains are making headway these days. But Karval's words are frightening all the same. 'At Chanteleine Castle,' he said. We have to get there soon."

"Yes! Yes!" replied the count, with sorrow and intense excitement in his voice. "But what about these poor people and the Catholic cause?"

"My lord," said Kernan gravely, "family comes before country. Without us, what would happen to Madame the Countess and my niece Marie? You have done your duty as a gentleman. You have fought for God and the King. Let's return to the castle, and once our family is safe, we'll come back. The Catholic Army has been destroyed, but all is not lost. Believe me, things are starting to move in the Morbihan. I know a man there named Jean Cottereau, who will make trouble for the Republicans, and we'll help him do it."

"Come on, then," said the count. "You're right. Karval's words are threatening. I have to take my wife and daughter out of France, and then I'll come back and get killed here."

"We'll come back together, my lord," replied Kernan.

"But how can we get to the castle?"

"In my opinion," said the peasant, "we should go to Guérande, follow along the coast either to Croisic Point or to Piriac, and from there go by sea to one of the bays in Finistère."

"But what will we do for a boat?"

"Have you got any gold on you?"

"Yes, nearly fifteen hundred *livres*."

"Well, with that we'll buy a fishing boat—and the fisherman too, if we have to."

"But…"

"We have no choice, my lord. By land we would soon run into a party of Blues, or we'd be forced to hide, to stay off the main roads and take the trails. We'd lose time walking back and forth and we might get there too late—if we got there at all."

"All right, then. Let's go," said the count.

"Let's go," replied Kernan.

The Count of Chanteleine had every confidence in Kernan, who was like a brother to him. The worthy Breton was like a member of his family. He called Marie de Chanteleine "my niece," and the girl referred to him as "my uncle Kernan." Since childhood, master and servant had never been separated. The Breton's education had raised him above the level of other people of his station in life. After sharing his childhood pleasures and youthful exertions with the count, he had also shared with him the misery and misfortunes of war. When the count left to join Cathelineau, he would have preferred leaving Kernan at Chanteleine Castle, but separating brother from brother would have been impossible. Other servants stayed behind, in any case, to protect the countess. Besides, he was reassured by the castle's location, at the end of Finistère, far from Quimper and Brest, where the Republican clubs were active, in a remote region between Le Fouesnant and Plougastel. Believing that his family was safe, he threw himself without hesitation into the Royalist movement.

The only immediate danger from which he had to flee stemmed from the meeting with Karval, and the threats and words of the former servant at the castle, who had been discharged a year before for stealing.

And so the count and Kernan left the main road just as the fugitives were coming to the Saint-Joachim marshes. They got a final glimpse of the terrified column as it disappeared in the darkness, its cries gradually dying out in the night..

At eight o'clock that evening, the count and Kernan reached Guérande. They were barely half an hour ahead of the swiftest of the fugitives. The town's portcullises were closed, but they entered the deserted streets through the rear gate.

What a gloomy silence, compared to the horrible din at Savenay! Not a light in any window, not a single belated passer-by. Terror kept the inhabitants shut up in the dark houses, behind barred and bolted doors. All morning, the people of Guérande had heard the cannon. Whatever the outcome of the battle, they could fear either an influx of defeated and desperate refugees or an invasion by the inflexible conquerors.

As the two fellow fugitives walked quickly over the irregular paving stones, their footsteps produced a sinister sound. They arrived at the church and were soon on the ramparts.

From there, they could hear the noise coming from the countryside and growing ever louder, a threatening murmur occasionally punctuated by the sound of gunfire.

The rain had stopped and the moon appeared through the dark, low-lying, scattered clouds, twisted by gusts of wind from the west. An optical illusion made the moon appear to be fleeing madly along, as if it were afflicted by vertigo. Its light was very bright at times, and its strong glare lit up the countryside, showing the smallest details with remarkable clarity and casting broad and rapidly moving shadows on the ground.

The count and Kernan turned their gaze out to sea. The Bay of Guérande opened out before them, beyond the immense checkerboard of the salt marshes. To the left, the clock tower of the village of Batz rose above the yellowish dunes. Farther on, the point of Croisic, showing indistinctly through the fog, formed the end of the tongue of land that disappeared into the ocean. To the right, at the end of the bay, Kernan's keen eyes could still make out the clock tower of Piriac. Farther on, the sea sparkled in the moonlight, blending seamlessly with the line of the sky.

The wind was blowing violently. The scrawny trees waved their leafless skeletons about, and from time to time a stone, dislodged from its socket, rolled down from the top of the ramparts into the muddy ditch below.

"Well," said the Count of Chanteleine to his companion, leaning into the wind. "There is Croisic Point and there is Piriac. Where shall we go?"

"At Croisic it would be easier to find a fishing boat, but if we had to back-track once we were on that tongue of land, we would be in a very difficult situation and it would be easy to cut off our retreat."

"We'll do as you say, Kernan. I'll follow you. But take the shortest route, even if it's not the safest."

"In my opinion, we should go round the bay and head for Piriac. It's barely three leagues from here, and if we keep up a good pace we'll be there is less than two hours."

"Let's go," replied the count.

The two fugitives left the town just as the first ranks of the Vendéans were coming in over the rampart on the opposite side, forcing their way through the gates, climbing over the ditches, launching a regular assault. Lights quickly appeared in the windows. The peaceful town of Guérande was filled with an unusual noise and disturbance. Its old walls were shaken by gunfire, and soon the church bell filled the air with the urgent sound of the alarm.

The count felt a violent pang of anguish. His hand clutched his musket, as if he were about to go back to the aid of his unfortunate companions.

"What about Madame the Countess?" said Kernan in a grave voice, "and my niece Marie?"

"Come on! Come on!" said the count, as he strode quickly down the slope leading from the town.

Soon master and servant were out in the countryside. They went down to the shore in order to avoid the usual route and skirted the salt marshes, whose little piles of salt sparkled in the moonlight. Sinister murmurs were coming through the scrawny trees that bent before the force of the sea wind. The melancholy sound of the rising tide was deafening.

Several times painful cries were heard. A stray bullet would strike a rock on the shoreline with a sharp sound. Flames cast their pale reflection on the horizon, and packs of famished wolves, smelling living flesh, filled the darkness with their sinister howls.

The count and Kernan walked along without exchanging a word, but they were both agitated by the same thoughts, which were communicated from one to the other as clearly as if they had been spoken.

Sometimes they stopped to look back and survey the countryside. Then, seeing that they were not being pursued, they resumed their onward march with long strides.

Before ten o'clock they reached the village of Piriac. Not wanting to risk going along its streets, they went on directly to Castelli Point.

From there they had a view of the open sea. To the right rose the rocks of Dumet Island; to the left the lighthouse of Le Four Island cast its intermittent flashes to every point on the horizon; farther out to sea lay the dark and shapeless mass of Belle Island.

Not seeing any fishing boats, the count and his companion returned to Piriac, where several small boats, anchored to the beach, were bobbing in the wave of the rising tide.

Kernan's glance caught one of them, which a fisherman, who had just furled his sail, was about to leave.

"Hey there, friend," he shouted to him.

The fisherman leaped out onto the beach and approached, looking rather worried.

"Come here," said the count.

The fisherman took a few steps forward. "You're not from around here," he said. "What do you want with me?"

"Could you put out to sea this very night," said Kernan, "and take us...?"

He stopped in mid-sentence.

"Where?" asked the fisherman.

"Where? We'll tell you that once we're on our way," said the count.

"The sea is rough and the sou'west wind is against us."

"We'll pay you well," replied Kernan.

"No one will ever pay me well enough to risk my hide," said the fisherman, trying to stare down the other two.

There was a pause, and he continued. "You're coming from the direction of Savenay, aren't you? Things are really humming out there!"

"What's that to you?" said Kernan. "Will you take us on board or not?"

"No, and that's final."

"Can we find a sailor in town who is more venturesome than you are?" asked the count.

"I doubt it," replied the fisherman. "But tell me," he added with a wink, "you're only saying half of what you need to say if you want to get on board. What will you pay me?"

"A thousand *livres*," replied the count.

"Worthless paper!"

"Gold," replied Kernan.

"Gold? Real gold? Let's have a look."

The count undid his belt and took out about fifty gold *louis*.

"Your boat isn't worth a quarter of that."

"Perhaps not," replied the fisherman, "but my skin is sure worth the rest."

"Well then."

"Get in," said the fisherman, taking the gold from the count.

He pulled the boat towards the shore. The count and Kernan waded in up to their knees and jumped in. The anchor was yanked out of the sand. Meanwhile, Kernan pulled on the halyard and the reddish foresail billowed in the wind.

Just as the fisherman was about to get on board, Kernan pushed him away vigorously. Then he took a gaffe and poled the vessel a dozen feet or so out to sea.

"Hey," said the fisherman.

"Keep your skin," Kernan shouted to him. "We don't need it. Your boat has been paid for."

"But..." said the count.

"I know what I'm doing," replied Kernan. Hauling on the mainsheet and holding the tiller, he brought the vessel about into the wind,

The dazed fisherman said not a word, and when he found his voice again, all he could do was shout, "Republican thieves!"

But the vessel was already disappearing into the darkness, among the foaming waves.

Chapter III

THE CROSSING

Kernan, as he had just said, had no difficulty sailing a small boat. He had shown his skill as a fisherman when he was a young man, and he had an intimate knowledge of the coast of Brittany from Croisic Point as far as Cape Finistère. There was not a rock that he did not know, not a cove nor a bay that he had not visited. He knew when the tides rose and when they fell, and reefs and shoals held no terrors for him.

The vessel the two fugitives were sailing was a narrow fishing boat, low at the stern but high in the bow, and marvelously well-suited to withstand the sea, even in heavy weather. It carried two red sails, a foresail and a lugsail.

The deck, which covered its entire length, had only one opening, designed for the helmsman. This enabled it to sail safely through the waves, as it often had to do when fishing sardines off Belle Island, or coming back to find the mouth of the Loire and sail upstream to Nantes.

It took both Kernan and the count to handle the boat, but once the sails were up it sailed off the wind.

Helped by the southwest wind, the boat skimmed quickly over the waves. Although there was a very strong breeze, the Breton had decided not to reef in his sails, which sometimes heeled over so far that the tack touched the water. But with a bold turn on the tiller, or by letting the mainsheet out a little, Kernan brought the boat upright again and headed into the wind.

At five o'clock in the morning they passed between Belle Island and the peninsula of Quiberon, which, a few months later, to England's shame, would be drenched in French blood.

The boat's stores, a small quantity of smoked fish, provided a little nourishment for the two fugitives, who had not eaten for more than fifteen hours.

During the first part of the crossing, the Count of Chanteleine said very little. He was in the grip of a powerful emotion. In his mind, scenes from the past mingled with those of the future. Hurrying to the aid of his wife and daughter, he pictured them as more and more gravely threatened. He considered the likelihood of a tragedy and tried to recall the last news he had had from the castle.

"That Karval," he said at last to Kernan, "is well known in the region, and if he showed up there, the people at the castle would certainly give him a very unpleasant reception."

"Yes indeed," replied the Breton. "They wouldn't miss a chance to rough him up. But if the scoundrel comes, he won't come alone, and besides, he only has to denounce Madame the Countess and my niece Marie and they will be arrested. Two poor harmless women! Oh! The times we're living through!"

"Yes, it's terrible, Kernan. These are times when the wrath of God falls on us, but we must submit to his will. The lucky ones are the people with no family, who only have themselves to be concerned about. As for us, Kernan, we're struggling, we're defending ourselves, we're fighting for a holy cause. But our mothers, our sisters, our daughters, and our wives can only weep and pray."

"Fortunately, we're here," replied Kernan, "and anyone who tries to get to them will have to kill us first. In any case, my lord, you did well to leave Madame and Mademoiselle at Chanteleine. The brave women wanted to follow you and take part in the campaign, just as Mme de Lescure, Mme de Donnissan, and so many others did. But at what cost in suffering and misery!"

"And yet," replied the count, "I'm sorry they aren't here with me. I would know they were safe, but after Karval's threats, I'm afraid."

"Tomorrow morning, if the wind is with us, we'll reach the coast of Finistère. Whatever happens then, we won't be far from the castle."

"They'll certainly be surprised to see us again, those poor women," said the count, with a sad smile.

"And happy, too," added Kernan. "My niece Marie will put her arms around her father's neck and fall into her uncle's arms. But we must get them to safety without wasting any time."

"Yes, you're right. The Blues will visit the castle before long, and the Municipality of Quimper will soon hear the alarm."

"So then, my lord, you know exactly what we will have to do when we get to the castle?"

"Yes," said the count, with a sigh.

"There are no two ways about it," continued the Breton, "we only have one choice."

"And that is…"

"Collect all your money together, my lord, and mine, find ourselves a ship, whatever it may cost, and escape to England."

"Emigrate!" said the count, in a pained voice.

"We must!" replied Kernan. "It's no longer safe in this country, either for you or for your family."

"You're right, Kernan. The Committee of Public Safety will carry out terrible reprisals in Brittany and in the Vendée. After their victory there will be a massacre."

"As you say. They have already sent their cruelest agents to Nantes and they'll send others to Quimper and Brest. The rivers of Finistère will be choked with dead bodies, just as the Loire was."

"Yes," replied the count. "My wife! My daughter! Saving them is our first priority, the poor, gentle souls! But if we emigrate, Kernan, you'll follow us."

"I'll rejoin you, my lord."

"You won't leave with us?"

"No. There's someone I have to settle accounts with before I leave Brittany."

"Karval?"

"Exactly."

"Forget about him, Kernan, he won't escape divine justice."

"My lord, I have an idea that he will begin with human justice."

The count knew how obstinate his servant was, and how difficult it would have been to make him abandon his plans for vengeance. He held his peace and, being both a father and a husband, directed all his thoughts toward his wife and child.

He scanned the coastline, counting the hours and the minutes, never thinking of the dangers the storm might have put in his way. All the horror of that civil war, with its frightful acts of cruelty on both sides, came back to him. Never had his wife and daughter seemed to be in such grave danger. In his mind's eye, he saw them being attacked and imprisoned, or perhaps fleeing, waiting among the rocks along the shore for some unexpected rescue. Sometimes he began to listen for a call to reach his ears.

"Don't you hear anything?" he asked Kernan.

"No," replied the Breton. "It's just a seagull caught in the storm."

At ten o'clock in the evening, Kernan recognized the entrance to the harbor of Lorient and the fort of Port-Louis, whose light was shining through the darkness. He set a course for the channel between the mainland and Groix Island and headed for the open sea.

The wind was still favorable, but was growing much stronger. Kernan, although he wanted to go quickly, and in spite of the count's impatience, had to take in all the reefs in his mainsail and lugsail. The count took the tiller himself, and the boat, without any apparent loss of momentum, ploughed through the foaming waves.

This dangerous voyage had lasted fifteen hours.

It was a dreadful night. The storm was raging furiously. The sight of the surf breaking against the granite rocks was enough to strike terror into the bravest hearts. The boat moved off shore to avoid the reefs that make the steep coast of Brittany so perilous.

The two fugitives could not get a single moment's sleep. One wrong turn on the tiller, or one careless moment, and their boat would capsize. They were struggling heroically and drawing fresh strength from the thought of the loved ones they were on their way to protect.

Around four o'clock in the morning the force of the hurricane subsided somewhat, and during a brief bright interval, Kernan could make out the position of Trévignon off to the eastward.

He could barely speak, but with his finger he pointed out the flickering gleam of the lighthouse. The count clasped his icy hands together, as if he were praying.

The boat now made for the bay of La Forêt, which extends from the village of Concarneau to Le Fouesnant.

The sea was calmer there, and the waves, protected from the on-shore winds, broke less heavily.

An hour later, the little craft crashed violently onto the rocks of Cape Coz. The impact was terrifying and unavoidable, even though the sails were down. The count and Kernan were flung into the water, but managed to get to shore, while the shattered boat sank before their eyes.

"There's nothing left," said Kernan to the count.

"It's just as well," was the reply.

"And now, on to the castle," said the Breton.

Their passage had taken twenty-six hours.

Chapter IV

Chanteleine Castle

Chanteleine Castle was located three leagues from the village of Fousenant, between Pont-l'Abbé and Plougastel, less than a league from the coast.

The lands making up the Chanteleine property had belonged to the count's family from time immemorial. His was one of the oldest families in Brittany. The castle dated back only to the time of Louis XIII, but it was marked with the rustic ruggedness that granite walls impart to buildings. It gave the impression of being heavy, imposing, but as indestructible as the rocks along the coastline. And yet, it had no towers, no machicolations, no rear entrance, no sentry box hanging like an eagle's nest from the corners of the walls, and it did not convey the idea of a fortress. In the peaceful land of Brittany, the seigneurs had never had to defend themselves against anyone, not even their vassals.

For many years the count's family had exercised an almost unquestioned feudal influence over the country. The Chanteleines were not exactly hangers-on at court, not being accommodating by nature, and in three hundred years they had not gone twice to pay their respects to the king. They considered themselves Bretons first and foremost, and separate from the rest of France. For them, the marriage of Louis XII and Anne of Brittany had never taken place, and they always resented that proud duchess for entering into what they openly called a "misalliance," or, even worse, an act of treason.

But while they reigned at home, the Chanteleines could be considered as models for the kings of France and could give them lessons in government. Besides, the proof of the pudding was in the eating; they were and always had been loved by their peasants.

This noble and highly esteemed family, very peaceful by nature, produced few illustrious captains. The Chanteleines were not born soldiers. In a period when donning a military uniform seemed to be the first duty of a gentlemen, they remained peacefully on their land, glad of the happiness they created around them. Since the time of Philippe Auguste, when the crusade (that is to say, the defense of their religion) took their ancestors off to the Holy Land, not a single Chanteleine had donned armor or buckled on a baldric. Needless to say, they were not well known at court, where they never asked any favors or made an effort to deserve them.

Their inherited property, wisely administered, had grown to a considerable size.

The Chanteleine property, with its meadows, salt marshes, and ploughed fields, was among the largest in the country, although it was unknown outside a radius of five or six leagues. Thanks to this situation, and although the surrounding communities of Le Fouesnant, Concarneau, and Pont-l'Abbé had already had a bloody visit from the Republicans of Brest and Le Finistère, Chanteleine Castle had escaped, as if by a miracle, the attention of the Municipalities when the count left it for the first time.

Although not warlike by nature, the count displayed considerable military talent during the Vendéan campaign. With faith and courage, one can be a soldier anywhere. For a man whose peaceful nature gave no indication of such an aptitude, the count conducted himself like a hero. Indeed, he had thought at first of a career in the church and had spent two years at the *grand séminaire* at Rennes. He was still pursuing his theological studies when his marriage to his cousin, Madamoiselle de la Contrie, set him on a totally opposite path.

But the count could not have found a more worthy partner to share his life. The attractive young woman became a courageous and devoted wife. The first years of the count and countess's marriage, with their daughter Marie to bring up, on this old family estate, among the servants, humble friends who had grown old in the service of the Chanteleine family, were as happy a time as anyone is ever permitted to spend in this world.

This happiness spread throughout the entire region, which held its seigneur in the greatest respect. The inhabitants considered themselves subjects of the count rather than of the king of France. This is understandable, since their relations with the king were always unpleasant, whereas the Chanteleine family came to their assistance on every occasion. Consequently, there was not an unhappy person or a beggar to be found in the whole region. Since time immemorial no crime had been committed in that remote part of Brittany. It is not surprising that Karval's thieving should have had such an effect, especially since he was a Breton himself. He had been in the count's service for two years when the latter was obliged to expel him from the castle. Actually, this action on his part only anticipated the justice that would have been meted out by the peasants, who would not have tolerated a thief in the region,

Yes, Karval was a Breton, but a Breton who had traveled and seen much of the country, including, no doubt, its ugly side. He was said to have visited Paris, which the peasants regarded as a fanciful place. To the most superstitious, it was the antechamber of hell. There must have been some truth in that, since the only one among them who had ever set foot there had come back a criminal.

This affair, which caused such a great scandal, had occurred two years earlier, and Karval had left the region uttering threats of vengeance. People shrugged their shoulders.

But while the actions of an obscure thief were beneath contempt, they could not be ignored when that thief had become one of the despicable and terrible agents of the Committee of Public Safety. The count, hurrying on towards the castle, was beginning to suspect that Karval's words hinted at sinister events. His wife's kindness, however, would surely protect her. For twenty years of her life, from 1773 to 1793, Madame de Chanteleine devoted herself entirely to the happiness of those who came to her. Since she knew that by doing good she made her husband happy, she was continually seen at the bedside of the ill, taking in old folk, providing instruction for children, and founding schools. Later, when Marie reached the age of fifteen, she was allowed to participate in all these charitable works.

United in the same spirit of charity, and accompanied by Abbé Fermont, the castle's chaplain, mother and daughter traveled through the villages along the coast, from Bay of La Forêt to Point Raz, offering

consolation and alms to the fishermen's families, who suffered so often from storms.

"Our mistress," the peasants called her.

"Our good lady," said the peasant women.

"Our good mother," repeated the children.

It is not hard to understand why everyone envied Kernan. Marie called him "uncle," and he referred to her as his niece. He was truly like a brother to the count.

When the count left the castle after the uprising at Saint-Florent, it was the first time he had been away from home, the first time he and the countess had been separated. It was painful for her, but Humbert de Chanteleine, driven by a sense of duty, left, and his courageous wife could only give her approval to his going.

During the first months of the war, the couple often received news of each other through loyal messengers, but the count could not get away from the Catholic Army even for a day to come and embrace his family. Pressing events always kept him at his post. For ten long months, he had not seen his loved ones. For three months, in fact, since the disasters at Granville, Le Mans, and Chollet, he had had no news from the castle.

His concern can be understood when, accompanied by the faithful Kernan, he returned to his ancestral domain. The emotion he felt when setting foot on the shore of Le Fouesnant is not hard to imagine. He was no more than two hours away from the embraces of his wife and the kisses of his daughter.

"Come on, Kernan, let's go," he said.

"Let's go," replied the Breton, "and quickly. That will warm us up."

A quarter of an hour later, master and servant walked through the village of Le Fouesnant, still sound asleep, and past the cemetery, which had been devastated during the last visit by the Blues.

The people of Le Fouesnant had been the first to oppose the Revolution, because of the blaspheming priests sent to them by the Municipalities. On July 19, 1792, three hundred of them, led by their justice of the peace, Alain Nédellec, fought in the village itself against the national guards of Quimper. They were crushed. The conquerors pastured their horses in the cemetery and set up their tents in the church. The next day three wagon loads of prisoners returned to Quimper. Alain Nédellec became Brittany's first martyr when he fell under the new instrument of death, which the Breton administrators called "the beheading machine," and for whose use the municipal prosecutor gave them carefully detailed instructions. Since then, the village had not recovered from its defeat.

"You can see that the Blues have been here," said Kernan. "Ruins and desecration."

The count did not answer, and headed across the long plains that go down to the sea. It was now six o'clock in the morning. A chill had followed the rain, and the earth was hard. It was still very dark over the deserted moors and the vast fields of gorse, unfit for cultivation. The puddles had frozen over, and the white-clad undergrowth had a petrified appearance.

As the fugitives moved farther away from the sea, a few thin trees could be seen here and there. Their pale skeletons, bending before the violent gusts from the west, stood out on the horizon.

Soon the plains gave way to fields of dark wheat, strengthened by drainage ditches and irrigation channels and separated by rows of squat oak trees. They had to make their way across the fields and go through a swinging gate, balanced by a heavy stone and overgrown with dry bramble bushes. Kernan opened it to let the count through and as the gate dropped back into place with a thud, a white sleet fell from the branches of the trees and rattled on the ground.

Then the count and his companion hurried along the narrow footpath stamped out between the furrows and the hedge bordering the field. Sometimes they ran in spite of themselves.

Around seven o'clock dawn began to break. The castle was no more than half a league away. The countryside seemed quiet and deserted—even suspiciously quiet. The count could not help noticing this strange silence.

"There's not a peasant to be seen, not a horse going to the meadow," he said, with anxiety in his voice.

"It's still early in the morning," replied Kernan, who was also struck by the appearance of the countryside, but did not want to frighten the count. "People get up late in December."

Just then they entered a large forest of tall pine trees. This vast stand of evergreens was part of the count's estate and was visible from far out to sea.

A mass of dry, grayish, unpeeled pine cones lay on the ground among the branches with their rough bark. It was evidently a long time since any human being had set foot here. And yet, every year the children from the surrounding villages used to come and joyfully gather these pine cones, and the housewives used them as a supply of firewood, with the count's generous permission.

This year, however, the poor folk had not made their usual collection, and the harvest of branches and dry cones was still untouched.

"You see," said the count to the Breton, "they didn't come. Neither the women nor the children."

Kernan shook his head without answering. He felt there was something unsettling in the air. His heart beat madly in his chest and he lengthened his stride.

As the two companions went on, hares, rabbits, and partridges sprang out from under their feet in great numbers—too great, in fact. Evidently there had not been many hunters that year, although everyone was free to hunt on the count's land.

There were unmistakable signs of abandonment and neglect. Despite the intense cold of that winter morning, the count's face turned pale.

"There's the castle at last," shouted the Breton, indicating the points of two turrets rising above a distant clump of trees.

At that point, the count and Kernan were close to the farm of La Bordière, occupied by one of the count's tenant farmers. They would see it once they rounded the woodlot. Louis Hégonec, the farmer, was an active man, an early riser and a rather noisy worker. But now his voice was not to be heard singing as he harnessed his oxen or his horses, or shouting to his old wife in the courtyard.

No, there was nothing. Everywhere a deathly silence reigned. The count, stricken with dreadful forebodings, had to take hold of the faithful Breton's arm for support.

As they came through the woodlot, their glance turned immediately towards the little farm.

A horrible sight met their eyes. A few fragments of shattered walls, blackened bits of beams, the end of a burned ridgepole, the remains of chimneys perched on top of a gable, narrow trails of soot snaking over the walls, broken doors, hinges sticking out like threatening fists between the stones, all the marks of a recent fire appeared at once. The trees bore the signs of a violent struggle. Marks of axe blows on the doors, bullet scars on the old oak trunks, broken and twisted farm equipment, overturned carts, rimless wheels, all bore witness to the violence of the battle. The abandoned bodies of cattle and horses polluted the air.

The count felt his legs giving way under him.

"The Blues! Always the Blues!" said Kernan in a dull voice.

The count uttered a terrible cry: "On to the castle!"

It was all Kernan could do to keep up with this man who, a few minutes earlier, could barely stand up.

As they hurried along, not a single human being appeared on the torn-up roads. The countryside was not simply empty; it was deserted.

The count walked through the village. Most of the houses had been burned; a few were still standing, but empty. A wave of vengeance must have passed through the village to depopulate it to that extent.

The Breton muttered between his teeth, "Karval! Karval!"

The count and Kernan finally came up to the castle door. The fire had spared it, but it was dark and silent. Not a single chimney sent its plume of morning smoke into the air.

The count and Kernan rushed towards the door and stopped, appalled.

"Look at that! Look at that!" said the count.

An enormous sign was pasted onto one of the door jambs. At the top it displayed the eye of the law and bundles of pikes and branches surmounted by the Phrygian bonnet, the emblem of the Revolution. On one side was a description of the property, on the other, its evaluation.

Chanteleine castle, had been confiscated by the Republic and was up for sale.

"The scoundrels!" exclaimed Kernan.

He tried to shake the door, but to no avail. For all his prodigious strength, it resisted obstinately. The count could not even have a moment's rest in his ancestral manor. His own door was shut against him. He was overcome by a terrible despair.

"My wife! My daughter!" he cried, in a tone that is impossible to describe. "Where is my wife? My child? They have killed them! They have killed them!"

Large tears rolled down Kernan's cheeks as he tried in vain to console his master.

"It's useless to keep pounding at this door," he said at last. "It won't open."

Just then, an old woman, who had been crouching in the ditch, stood up all of a sudden. To the eyes of anyone less dismayed, she would have been a painful sight. Her foolish head bobbled stupidly.

The count ran up to her.

"Where is my wife?" he asked.

With great effort, the old woman replied, "She died in the attack on the castle."

"She's dead!" screamed the count.

"And what about my niece?" asked Kernan, shaking the old woman vigorously.

"In prison in Quimper," she said at last.

"Who did that?" asked Kernan in a furious voice.

"Karval," replied the old woman.

"On to Quimper!" shouted the count. "Come, Kernan, come!"

And they left the unfortunate woman, alone and almost breathing her last. She was the only living being left in the village of Chanteleine.

Chapter V

QUIMPER IN 1793

Quimper had seen the first head fall under the Republican axe, the head of Alain Nédellec. In that town also, the Breton clergy mourned its first martyr, Bishop Conen de Saint-Luc. From that day on, Quimper was controlled by the despotism of the Republicans and the Municipality.

It must be said that Republican fury was the distinguishing trait of the urban population of Brittany. They flung themselves headlong into the national movement. Their energetic nature, both for good and evil, knew no bounds. So it was that the first heroes of August 10, who stormed the Tuileries and overthrew King Louis XVI, were the "federalists" of Brest, Morlaix, and Quimper. They were aroused by the voice of the Legislative Assembly, which declared on July 11, 1792, when Prussia, Piedmont, and Austria formed a coalition against France, "The fatherland is in danger."

Their services were so highly appreciated that the Breton Club of Paris formed the nucleus of the future Jacobin Club. Later on, the section from the suburb of Saint-Marceau adopted the title of Section du Finistère in their honor.

Quimper was one of the hotbeds of the revolution, contrary to what one might have expected of this county seat hidden away in Lower Brittany. The Friends of the Constitution was founded there and made its headquarters in the former Chapelle des Cordeliers. The clubs grew in number and one of them later decreed that suckling babes should leave their nurses' breasts to come and hear the shouts of *Vive la Montagne,* and that children should learn to speak by babbling the Declaration of the Rights of Man.

However, when the administrators of Quimper, headed by Kergariou, saw the turn events were taking and the direction in which the Revolution was going, they wanted to stamp out the movement. They banned certain newspapers, such as Marat's *L'Ami du Peuple.* The Paris Commune sent a proconsul to bring them into line, but when he arrived, the people of Quimper locked him up in the Fort du Taureau, and protested, even more vigorously than the Girondins of Paris did, against the "montagnards" of the Convention. They even joined with Nantes to send two hundred armed volunteers to Paris to support their protest. This led to charges being laid against all the local administrations of Brittany. But after the death of Louis XVI and the execution of the Girondins, when France was tottering on the brink and the Reign of Terror was setting in, the reactionary Republicans in Brittany were swamped with work.

But while the townspeople had supported the movement, the rural areas distinguished themselves first of all by their resistance to the appointment of priests who had taken the oath of loyalty. They

drove them away in disgrace. Then, when the conscription law was passed, it became very difficult to hold back the peasants in Finistère, Le Morbihan, Loire-Inférieure, and Côtes-du-Nord. General Canclaux had all he could do to keep them down with his army and the municipal militia. On March 19, he even had to fight a pitched battle at Saint-Pol-de-Léon.

The Committee of Public Safety then decided to act against the towns and rural areas with the utmost severity. It sent two delegates, Guermeur and Jullien, who organized the "sans-culottes" movement in Brittany, and especially in Quimper.

These proconsuls brought with them the Law on Suspects, passed in September, 1793. It had been drafted by Merlin, of Douai, and read as follows:

> "The following are regarded as suspects:
> "1. Those who, by their behavior, by their associations, by their words or writings, have shown themselves to be supporters of tyranny and federalism, and enemies of liberty.
> "2. Those who cannot account for their life-style or justify their enjoyment of civic rights.
> "3. Those who have been refused a certificate of civic-mindedness.
> "4. Civil servants who have been suspended or discharged from their functions.
> "5. Former members of the nobility, including the husbands, wives, fathers, mothers, sons, daughters, brothers, sisters, and agents of émigrés, who have not constantly demonstrated their support for the Revolution."

Armed with this law, the Committee of Public Safety's delegates were in control of the department. Who could hope to escape those revolutionary measures? There was no one who was not more or less directly implicated by those fearsome articles. Reprisals were carried out speedily, and all of Finistère was in the grip of the most extreme terror.

Guermeur and Jullien were accompanied by an assistant agent of the committee, an insignificant person who was none other than the accursed Karval, against whom Kernan had sworn vengeance.

This scoundrel had been active in Paris, and had attracted attention in the clubs. He had infiltrated the ranks of the terrorists and accompanied the delegates, claiming to have a special knowledge of the department of Finistère.

In fact, he was coming to wreak his despicable vengeance on the region that had driven him out. Armed with this Law on Suspects, it was not difficult for him to gain access to the Chanteleine family.

The day after he arrived in Quimper, he made ready to act.

Karval was a man of medium height, with the kind of face that is produced over time by hatred, pettiness, and meanness. Every new vice sank in and left its mark. He was not lacking in intelligence, but one had the impression, on seeing him, that he must be a coward. Like many heroes of the Revolution, he was blood-thirsty out of fear, but out of fear also he was inflexible and without human feeling.

On September 14, the day after his arrival, he went to see Guermeur.

"Citizen," he said, "I need a hundred militiamen."

"What do you want them for?"

"I've got a score to settle back where I came from."

"Where's that?"

"Over by the Chanteleine estate, between Plougastel and Pont-l'Abbé. I know there's a nest of Vendéans there."

"Are you sure of what you're saying?"

"I'm sure. Tomorrow I'll bring you the father and the mother."

"Don't let the kids get away," replied the fierce proconsul with a laugh.

"Don't worry, I know what I'm doing. I've cleaned out bird's nests before, and I want to teach them to whistle *Ça ira!*"

"Go ahead, then," said Guermeur, and he signed the order that Karval requested.

"A fraternal good-bye to you!" said Karval as he left. The next day, he set out with his detachment, made up of fanatics from the town. They reached the Chanteleine estate the same day.

The peasants knew Karval well, and when they saw him they put up a desperate struggle. They realized it was a case of do or die, but after trying to defend their "good lady," they were defeated.

The Countess of Chanteleine, along with her daughter, Abbé Fermont, and her servants, suffered agonies as they waited for the outcome of the battle.

She did not have long to wait. The Quimper militiamen seized the castle, and Karval led them into the apartments, shouting, "Death to the nobles! Death to the Whites! Death to the Vendéans!"

The distraught countess tried to escape, but there was not enough time. The fanatics caught up with her in the castle chapel, where she had taken refuge.

"Arrest that woman and her daughter, the wife and daughter of a criminal," shouted Karval, drunk with blood and joy, "and that man in the skullcap too," he added, pointing to Abbé Fermont.

Marie had fainted in her mother's arms, and was dragged away.

"Where is your husband, the count?" demanded Karval in a fierce voice.

The countess looked at him proudly, but did not answer.

"And where is Kernan?" he shouted.

Again silence. He was enraged to see that the two men had escaped, and in his anger he struck the countess a mortal blow. The poor woman fell to the ground, casting a last anguished glance at her daughter. Karval looked everywhere, but in vain.

"They're with the army of criminals," he cried. "All right! I'll find them."

Then, turning to his men, he said. "Take that girl away. That's something, anyway."

The unconscious Marie was placed among the peasants who had been arrested, along with Abbé Fermont. Their hands were tied and they were led away, herded together like cattle.

The next day, Karval brought his prisoners to Guermeur.

"What about the male?" said Guermeur with a laugh.

"He flew away. But don't worry," replied Karval with a hideous smile. "I'll nab him."

Marie de Chanteleine and her unfortunate companions were flung pell-mell into the town jails. The young woman did not regain consciousness until she was behind bars.

But eventually the prisons became too small. In the attempt to empty them, the death machine worked ceaselessly on the main square of Quimper. There was even talk of setting it up in the court itself, in order to speed matters up.

The way revolutionary justice was carried out during the Terror is well known, what formalities were observed and what guarantees were offered to the accused.

The unfortunate young woman's turn could not be far off.

That was what had occurred in the two months when the Count of Chanteleine had been without news of his wife and daughter. Those were the frightful scenes that had taken place at his castle.

Now Kernan understood the air of satisfied vengeance that showed on Karval's face when, in the midst of the battle, he shouted out those terrible words: "We'll be waiting for you at Chanteleine Castle."

And so, as he walked along, supporting his master, who was crushed by the disaster, he kept murmuring, "I'll have no mercy on you, Karval, no mercy!"

It was nearly eight o'clock when the count and Kernan left the castle. Neither hunger nor weariness could delay them for a single moment. As they hurried across the fields, the Breton looked back one last time and saw, behind the bare trees, the walls of his master's castle.

The count, nearly mad with grief, was guided by his faithful servant, who took on enough courage and intelligence for them both. In order to avoid any unpleasant encounter, he took the cross roads and soon rejoined the main highway from Concarneau to Quimper at the village of Kerrolland.

The count and Kernan were now no more than two and a half leagues from Quimper, and the rate at which they were walking would bring them there before ten o'clock in the morning.

"Where is she? Where is my daughter?" murmured the count, who would have aroused pity in the hardest of hearts. "She's dead! Dead! Like her poor mother."

Gloomy and terrifying visions filled his mind. In order to dispel them, he began to run, as if he had not seen them.

Kernan stayed with him, following him in his mad leaps and even making him dive into the bushes when some passer-by appeared far down the road. Any man might be dangerous under such circumstances, and in the count's agitated state, he would have given himself away.

The Breton was certainly suffering as much as his master, but at the same time he was mulling over plans for revenge that the count did not dream of. His grief was mingled with a great surge of anger. Then he began to reflect, asking himself questions to which he had no answer. What was the count going to do in the town?

If his daughter was in prison, would he manage to get her back? Revolutionary justice never gave up its prey, and the count himself would be arrested if he made the slightest suspicious move.

And so, without any definite plan or preconceived idea, the two men walked on aimlessly, driven by some invincible power.

As Kernan had predicted, they reached the suburbs of Quimper before ten o'clock. The streets were almost deserted, but a kind of ominous murmur could be heard in the distance. The entire populace seemed to have gathered near the center of town. Kernan went boldly through the streets, restraining his master, who kept repeating in a low voice, "My daughter! My child!"

It was the father who was suffering, even more than the husband. There was no cure for his grief.

A ten-minute walk brought master and servant to one of the streets close to the cathedral, where they found themselves at the back of a large crowd.

Some people were screaming and shouting. Others were retreating in terror to their houses and closing the doors and windows. Cries of grief were mingled with curses. Terror-stricken faces appeared side by side with blood-thirsty faces. There was something sinister in the air.

Soon, in the midst of the tumult, these words could be heard: "There they are! There they are!"

But neither the count not Kernan could see what was arousing the crowd's curiosity. The words were followed at once by prolonged shouts: "Down with the Whites! Down with the aristocrats! Long live the Republic!"

Obviously, something frightful was happening on the nearby square. At a turn in the street, every face was turned towards the same point, and most of them, it must be said, displayed inhuman passions, as they were coming to find their cruel satisfaction in this spectacle.

From time to time more violent murmurs could be heard. At one point, something extraordinary seemed to be taking place on the square, for the words "No! No mercy! No mercy!" spoken, or rather howled, by the people who could see, drifted back to the last rows of spectators.

The count's face broke out into a cold sweat.

"What's happening?" people were asking around him.

And without knowing, but prompted by a ferocious instinct, others shouted, "No mercy! No mercy!"

Kernan and the count wanted at all costs to force their way through the crowd, but their efforts were in vain. In any case, a few minutes after their arrival, the spectacle came to an end, for the crowd suddenly began to move back. Arms waved in the air, faces turned around, and the cries of rage gradually died out.

Then the town criers appeared, shouting out to the crowd the names of the victims.

"Execution on the 6th of Nivôse, Year II of the Republic. Who wants the list of the condemned?"

The count looked at Kernan with panic in his eyes.

"There! There!" continued the criers. "The priest Fermont."

The count squeezed Kernan's hand as if he would crush it.

"The Demoiselle de Chanteleine."

The count uttered a terrible cry. "Ah!"

But Kernan put his hand over his mouth, took him in his arms as he was fainting, and, before any witnesses could understand what was happening, dragged his master into a side street.

Meanwhile, other names were being shouted out to the crowd, and the cry rang out on all sides, "Death to the aristocrats! Long live the Republic!"

Chapter VI

THE INN OF THE EGALITARIAN TRIANGLE

Kernan was in a dreadful position. He had to get the count out of sight before he regained consciousness, since his first words would be certain to betray him. He would ask in a loud voice to have his daughter back, and that would expose him as the Count of Chanteleine in the garb of a Breton peasant.

As he was wandering through the streets, Kernan spotted a sort of inn and stopped in front of it, dragging, or rather carrying, his master.

The inn had a sign decked out with all the charming decorations of the time, such as the pikes and Roman fasces, and the words:

The Egalitarian Triangle
PROPRIETOR: MUTIUS SCEVOLA
Travelers on foot and on horseback welcome

"This is an inn for bandits," he said to himself. "All right! We'll be safer there. Besides, I have no choice."

He had little choice indeed. He would not have found a single tavern in town without its civic sign.

He went into the lower hall, set his inert burden down on a chair, and asked for a room. The innkeeper, Mutius Scévola, arrived in person.

"What do you want, citizen?" he asked the Breton in a gruff voice.

"A room."

"And you'll pay?"

"Of course!" replied Kernan. "We didn't rob the *Chouans* for nothing. Here, I'll pay in advance," he added, tossing a few coins on the table.

"Real money!" said the innkeeper, who was more accustomed to seeing paper money than metal.

"And good money, too, with the Republic's face on it."

"All right, we'll look after you. But what's the matter with your friend?"

"He's my brother, if that's not too much for you to swallow. As we were whipping our old nag, trying to get here on time…"

"For the execution!" said the innkeeper, rubbing his hands together.

"Exactly," replied Kernan without batting an eyelid. "We took a tumble into the ditch. The horse was killed on the spot, and this guy here is not in much better shape. But that's enough talking for now. I've paid you. Where's my room?"

"All right! All right! We'll take care of you. You don't have to get nasty about it. It's not my fault if you got here too late. But since you missed the execution of the criminals, I'll give you the details."

"You were there?"

"I sure was! Two steps away from Citizen Guermeur."

"He's quite a guy, he is," retorted Kernan, who had never even heard the name before.

"You can say that again!" replied the innkeeper.

"Well, so long for now, Citizen Scévola."

Scévola took the Breton, who had picked up his burden again, up to the third floor.

"Will you be needing me?" he asked, when they got there.

"No, not you or anyone else," replied the Breton.

"He's not very polite, but he pays," muttered Scévola. "That's something, anyway."

A few moments later, Kernan was alone with the unconscious count, and could finally give way to his tears. But even as he was weeping, he took the greatest care of his master. He moistened his pale brow and managed to bring him back to consciousness. But he took the precaution of putting his hand over the count's mouth to stop the first outpouring of his grief.

"Yes, my lord," he said. "Let's weep, but let's weep silently. We aren't allowed to moan here."

"My wife! My daughter!" the count repeated between sobs. "Is it true, then? Is it possible? Dead! Murdered! And I was there! And I couldn't... Ah! I'll find their murderer!"

The count was thrashing about like a madman. Despite his herculean strength, Kernan had great difficulty controlling him and smothering his cries.

"My lord," he said, "you'll get yourself arrested."

"What do I care?" repeated the count as he struggled.

"You'll be guillotined!"

"So much the better! So much the better!"

"And so will I!"

"You! You!" said the count, sinking back into a state of profound prostration.

For a few minutes, his chest heaved with heavy sobs. Finally he calmed down, knelt on the bare floor of the room, and prayed for his lost loved ones.

Kernan knelt down beside him and added his tears to those of the count. After a long prayer, he stood up and said, "Now, my lord, let me go through the town. You stay here, pray and weep. I have to find out what has happened."

"Kernan, you will tell me everything that you learn," replied the count, taking his servant's hands.

"Everything, my lord. I swear it! But you will not leave this room?"

"I promise. Go now, Kernan."

The count put his head down in his hands again, and large tears welled out between his fingers.

Kernan went back down to the lower hall and found Scévola at the door.

"Well," asked the patriotic innkeeper, "how's your brother?"

"He's sleeping. It's nothing serious, but I don't want him to be disturbed. Is that clear?"

"Don't worry."

"Now," said Kernan, "I'm listening."

"Ah! You want me to tell you the story. Yes, I thought you would," he added with a laugh. "You got in line, but you couldn't get in. There were too many people."

"Exactly."

"But can you listen without drinking, citizen? I can't talk without something to moisten my words."

"All right, bring out a bottle," said Kernan, "and a loaf of bread too. I'll listen to you while I'm having a bite to eat."

"Right you are," replied Mutius Scévola.

A moment later, the two men were sitting at a table and Citizen Scévola was doing the honors for his benefit.

"Here's what happened," he said, after he had downed a glass of wine. "For two months, the town's prisons had been bursting at the seams. Many of the prisoners were escapees from the Vendée, and we could see the time coming when we wouldn't be able to take any more prisoners for lack of prisons. So we had to empty them—and fast. Unfortunately, Citizen Guermeur is a good patriot, but he hasn't got the imagination of Carrier or Le Bon. He wanted to go by the book."

Kernan was clenching his fists under the table as he heard those words, but he had enough self-control not only to hold himself back, but also to answer, "Carrier. Now there's a good man!"

"Yes, you can say that again. With his drowning parties! And besides, he has such a beautiful river available to him. Anyway, we did what we could for two months. We proceeded province by province. The aristocrats couldn't complain, because all the provinces were dying together. Finally, we worked so well that we nearly succeeded in emptying the prisons. But people kept filling them up again."

"And this morning," asked Kernan, "didn't they execute Mademoiselle de Chanteleine, the aristocrat?"

"Yes, a pretty slip of a girl, upon my word. And her priest with her, to show her the way. It was Karval who pulled that one off."

"Ah! The famous Karval?"

"That's the one. There's a guy who's going places. Do you know him?

"Do I know him? We're old friends. We're like two fingers on the same hand," Kernan replied calmly. "Is he here?"

"No, he left a week ago to make a tour. I have to tell you that he didn't get the job finished. When he attacked Chanteleine, he hoped to arrest the former count. He had something in mind for him. But the bird had flown."

"Then what?" asked Kernan.

"Then he rejoined Kléber's army, thinking he could nab his man, and I wouldn't be surprised if he succeeded during the rout at Savenay."

"That's possible, because we really clobbered the Whites there," replied the Breton. "But tell me, what about the girl?"

"What girl?"

"The aristocrat from this morning. How did she react?"

"Bah! Not too well," replied the innkeeper, raising his glass to his lips. "There wasn't much fun to be had with her. She was half dead with fear."

Kernan could hardly contain himself. "So," he said, "she's really dead, then?"

"She sure is—unless she had a secret," laughed the innkeeper. "But you know, something strange happened during the ceremony."

"And what was that, Citizen Scévola?" asked Kernan. "You're very interesting."

"Yes, I am," boasted the monster, "But I'm going to say something now that I'd rather not have to tell you."

"And why not?"

"Because it looks bad for the Committee of Public Safety."

"What? The Committee?"

"One of its members showed mercy."

"And who was that?"

"The virtuous Couthon."

"Impossible!"

"Judge for yourself. This morning, the guillotine was calmly working away. Peasants, nobles, priests, all of them were toppling over with true Republican equality. The Chanteleine girl had had her turn, and there were only two or three condemned prisoners left, when a noise broke out in the crowd. A young man with his hair all disheveled, riding a horse that fell dead on the spot, ran up, shouting, 'Mercy! Have mercy on my sister!' He broke through the crowd, went up to Citizen Guermeur, and handed him a paper signed 'Couthon,' which granted a pardon to his sister."

"Well?"

"Well, there was no way around it. And yet, that lad was an aristocrat."

"And his name?"

"The Chevalier de Trégolan, I was told."

"I don't know him," replied Kernan.

"He walked right up to the guillotine, and that had a strange effect on him, for he lifted his arms in despair. You would have thought he was going to faint, he was so squeamish. But it was a good thing for him that he hadn't wasted any time, because his sister was already going up the steps, in a faint, on the arm of the citizen executioner. 'My sister! My sister!' he cried out. And they had to give her to him. So if his horse had lost its footing along the way, it would have been all over."

"And that's what caused the disturbance in the crowd?"

"Yes. People were shouting, 'No! No!' But Guermeur, when he saw the signature of the virtuous Couthon, had to go along with it. All the same, it's a black mark against the Committee of Public Safety."

"Well," replied Kernan, "he got a lucky break, that Trégolan. Then what happened?"

"Then he took his sister away, and we went on with our work."

"Well, here's to your health, Scévola," said Kernan.

"And to yours, mate," replied the innkeeper.

The two men clinked glasses.

"What are you going to do now?" asked the patriot.

"I'm going to see if my brother is still asleep and then I'm going to take a walk around town."

"As you wish. Feel free."

"Don't worry. I will."

"Are you planning to stay here for some time?"

"I would have liked to see Karval and shake hands with him," replied Kernan casually.

"But he may come back to Quimper any day now."

"If I was sure of that, I'd wait," said the Breton.

"Sorry. That's all I can tell you."

"Anyway," said the Breton, "I'll find him one of these days."

"Good!"

"Is he staying with you here?"

"No, he's living at the bishop's palace, with Citizen Guermeur."

"All right. I'll go and see him."

With that, Kernan left the innkeeper. The effort he had made to contain himself during this whole conversation had worn him out to the point where he could hardly climb the stairs.

"Yes, Karval," he repeated. "I'll catch up with you."

It is impossible to convey his tone of voice as he spoke those words.

When he finally went back to the count, he found him absorbed in grief, but resigned. Kernan had to tell him everything he had learned. After making sure that no one could hear him, after checking the walls, he told his melancholy tale in a low voice, while the tears kept running down the count's anguished face.

Then Kernan reminded him of what still had to be done.

"I have lost my wife and my child," replied the count. "There is nothing for me to do now but die, and I will die for the holy cause."

"Yes," said Kernan. "We'll go to Anjou and join the *Chouans*. They're getting restless."

"We'll go."

"Today."

"Tomorrow. I have one last duty to perform this evening."

"And what is that, my lord?"

"I want to go to the cemetery and pray over the common grave where they threw the body of my child."

"But…," said Kernan.

"That is what I want to do," replied the count in a soft voice.

"We'll pray together," said the Breton quietly.

They wept for the rest of the day. The two unfortunate men, clasping hands, were only aroused from their melancholy silence by the songs and demonstrations of joy that rang out in the street.

The count did not move. Nothing could distract him. Kernan went over to the window and almost uttered a terrible cry, but he controlled himself, and would not tell the count what he had just seen.

Karval, accompanied by his bloody mob, was entering Quimper, hideous, blood-stained, nearly drunk, driving before him the elderly, the wounded, women, children, and unfortunate Vendéan prisoners, plucked out of the routed grand army and now on their way to the scaffold.

He was on horseback, and all the criminals in the city were following him, hailing him with noisy cheers.

Karval was definitely becoming a person of some standing.

When he was gone, Kernan went up to the count and said to him in a low voice, "You are right, my lord. This is not the day for us to leave."

Chapter VII

THE CEMETERY

Evening came. The weather had changed to snow. At eight o'clock the count stood up and said, "It's time, let's go."

Without replying, Kernan opened the door and led the way. He hoped to avoid meeting Scévola, but the innkeeper heard them come down and, prompted by some instinct common to his trade, left the lower hall and stood by as the Breton was going out.

"Ah!" he said, "You're leaving, citizen?"

"Yes. My brother is feeling better."

"It's bad weather for starting on a journey. Couldn't he wait till tomorrow?"

"No," replied Kernan, who didn't know quite what to say.

"By the way," said Scévola, "you know that the virtuous Karval is back in Quimper?"

"Exactly," said the Breton. "We're going to the bishop's palace to visit him."

As he said those words, he turned towards the count, who fortunately had not heard that dreaded name.

"Ah! You're going to see him at the bishop's palace?" said the innkeeper.

"Yes, and I can assure you that he won't be upset by our visit."

"Ha ha!" said Scévola with a coarse laugh. "You're going to denounce some priests or émigrés, are you?"

"Perhaps," said Kernan, taking his master's arm and drawing him towards the door.

"Well, good luck to you, citizen."

"Good-bye," replied the Breton.

And they finally left the inn.

The town seemed deserted. A deep silence reigned in the snow-covered streets.

The two men kept close to the houses, the count following Kernan's lead. He did not notice the cold. Since making his decision to go and pray at his daughter's grave, he had not spoken a word and had become completely absorbed in his grief, Kernan respected his silence.

Twenty minutes later the walls of the cemetery appeared through the gloom. At that hour the gates were closed, but that made little difference, since the Breton had no intention of going in through the public entrance, where he would be seen by the attendant.

He walked around the walls, looking for a spot where he could climb over. The count followed him obediently, like a child or a blind man.

After a long search, he came to a place where the foundations of the wall had been laid bare and had partially collapsed, leaving an opening large enough to get through. Kernan darted up onto the stones, which were loosely held in place by a mixture of snow and mud. From there, he held out a hand to his master and they both went into the cemetery.

The whiteness of the resting-place presented a sorry sight to the eyes. A few tombstones and many black wooden crosses were covered by the white shroud of winter. It was a sad spectacle, this cemetery in mourning. One could not help thinking that the poor dead people must be very cold under that icy earth, and especially those whom an indifferent Municipality had just flung into a common grave.

Kernan and the count walked along a number of deserted paths until they came to a pit that had been barely filled in and was covered with irregular lumps that stood out clearly in the snow. The gravediggers' spades and picks were there, ready for the next day's work.

As he approached, Kernan thought he saw a human form crouching on the ground. It suddenly stood up and tried to hide behind the dark foliage of the cypress trees. At first he thought his eyes were causing him to hallucinate.

"I must be mistaken," he said to himself. "Someone here at this hour? It's impossible."

But as he watched closely, he saw the form moving under the trees. At the same time, he noticed fresh footprints. Someone had obviously just run away.

Was it a gravedigger making his rounds? A custodian? A grave robber?

Kernan held up his hand to stop the count. He waited a few moments and then, since the individual had not reappeared, walked towards the common grave.

"This is the place, my lord," he said.

The count knelt down on the icy earth, took off his hat, and began to pray and weep. His hot tears melted the snow as they fell to the ground.

Kernan was kneeling and praying too, but he was also watching and studying the surroundings.

Alas for the Count of Chanteleine! He would have liked to scrape away with his bare hands the earth that was hiding his child from him, to see her beloved features one last time, and give her mortal remains a more fitting burial place. He plunged his hands into the snow, uttering heart-rending sighs.

He stayed like that for a quarter of an hour. Kernan did not dare interrupt his grief, but he was afraid the count's sobs might be overheard by some lurking spy.

Just then he thought he heard footsteps. He turned around anxiously, and this time he distinctly saw a human form leaving the cypress grove and heading towards the grave.

"Ah!" said the Breton. "If this is a spy, he'll get what's coming to him."

Knife in hand, he rushed towards the stranger, who made no move to avoid him. On the contrary, he seemed to be ready and waiting for his attacker. Soon the two men were within three paces of each other, both assuming a defensive stance.

"What have you come here for?" asked the Breton abruptly.

The stranger, a young man of about thirty, wearing peasant clothing, replied in a voice filled with emotion, "The same as you."

"To pray?"

"To pray."

"Ah!" said Kernan. "You have relatives...?"

"Yes," replied the young man in a sorrowful voice.

The Breton looked at him closely and saw that he had tears in his eyes.

"Forgive me," he said. "I took you for a spy. Come."

With the stranger following him, he returned to the count, who, aroused from his torpor, was about to get to his feet when the young man motioned to him not to bother.

"You have come to pray, sir?" asked the count. "There is room for both of us on this grave. I am a father mourning for his child. They killed her this morning and threw her here."

"My deepest sympathy!" said the young man.

"But who are you?" asked Kernan.

"The Chevalier de Trégolan," was the instant reply.

"The Chevalier de Trégolan!" exclaimed Kernan.

He was immediately on his guard and resumed his attitude of defiance, for the name reminded him of what had gone on that morning, and he could not understand what the young man was doing in the cemetery.

"Yes," replied the chevalier.

"Are you the one who obtained a pardon for your sister this morning, and saved her?"

"Saved!" said the young man, clasping his hands together.

"And she is the one you have come here to weep for?"

"Chevalier," said the count, who was in no doubt, "you have been more fortunate than I. I arrived too late to see my child for the last time."

"Who are you, then?" asked the young man eagerly.

Kernan was about to rush over to his master to prevent him from speaking and revealing the secret of his name, when the latter announced gravely, "I am the Count of Chanteleine."

"You!" exclaimed the young man. "You are the Count of Chanteleine?"

"I am, sir."

"Good heavens!" said the stranger, grasping the count's hands and peering into his face.

"Well then?" asked Kernan impatiently.

"Come," said the young man quickly. "There is not a moment to lose."

"Just a minute," said Kernan. "Where are you planning to take my lord?"

"Come with me!" exclaimed the young man, with a note of violence in his voice.

The Breton was about to rush at the chevalier, who had taken the count's arm and was trying to drag him away, when the count said, "Let's go, Kernan, let's go. This is an honest man."

Kernan obeyed, taking his place at the young man's left, ready to strike him at the first sign of betrayal. They went out through the breach in the cemetery and walked along the walls. The Chevalier de Trégolan did not speak, but maintained his grip on the count's arm.

They went back into the town and disappeared into the narrow alleyways, instead of following the main streets. There was not another soul to be seen, but Kernan glanced attentively about him all the same.

The silence of the night was disturbed only once, when the chevalier and his two companions approached the bishop's palace. Shouts of joy were coming from its brightly lit windows. They were celebrating Karval's return. Judges and executioners alike were singing and dancing, and Kernan felt a terrible rage rise up in his heart.

Finally the young man stopped in front of a quiet, isolated house on the outskirts of a suburb.

"There it is," he said.

He walked up to door and was about to knock, but Kernan seized his arm as he was taking hold of the knocker.

"Just a minute," he said.

"Leave him alone, Kernan," said the count.

"No indeed, my lord. In these troubled times, any house is suspect. We have to know where we're going. Why are you taking us into this house?" he said, staring fixedly at the young man.

"To show you my sister," he replied with a sad smile.

He knocked lightly on the door. There was the sound of frightened steps approaching along the hallway, and then silence. The chevalier knocked again in a particular way and said, "For God and the King."

The door opened. An old woman was standing there. She seemed worried at seeing the young man accompanied by two strangers.

"These are friends," he said. "There is nothing to be afraid of."

The door closed quickly. By the light of a candle Kernan could catch a glimpse of a circular wooden staircase at the end of the hallway. The chevalier went up, followed by the count and the Breton, who was still armed.

He must have been reassured, however, by the words exchanged between the old woman and the young man.

"Chevalier," she said, "I was so worried while you were away."

"And what about her?" he asked.

"She's weeping pitifully," replied the old lady.

"Come, my lord count," said the young man.

At the top of the stairway there was a door with a ray of light shining out from under it. The chevalier threw it open and said simply, "My lord Count of Chanteleine, here is my sister!"

Pushing past the count, Kernan cast a quick glance around the interior of the room and uttered a cry, a frightening cry of surprise.

Mademoiselle de Chanteleine, Marie, his niece, was there before his eyes, lying on a bed, but alive! Alive!

"My child!" exclaimed the count.

"Ah! My father!" said the young woman, getting up and throwing herself into his arms.

It was an indescribably delirious moment. How could anyone have portrayed the caresses exchanged by the father and his daughter? Kernan kissed Marie and then went off into a corner to weep. The Chevalier de Trégolan clasped his hands as he watched the touching scene.

Suddenly Marie uttered a cry, as a terrible thought came to her mind.

"My mother!" she cried.

She was unaware that her mother had perished during the destruction of the castle.

Without a word, the count pointed heavenward, and his daughter fell back on the bed, almost in a faint.

"My daughter! My daughter!" said the count, hurrying to her side.

"Don't be afraid, my lord," said Kernan, as he raised the young woman's head. "This attack will pass."

And indeed, after a few moments, Marie regained consciousness and wept copiously. At last her sobs subsided, and the count was able to ask her some questions.

"By what miracle did you escape death, my child?" he asked.

"I don't know, father. I was dragged half dead onto the scaffold. I saw nothing. I heard nothing. The next thing I knew, I was here."

"Tell us what happened, Monsieur de Trégolan. Tell us," said the count.

"My lord," said the chevalier, "my sister had been thrown into jail in Quimper. In despair, I hurried to Paris, and after much pleading. I obtained a pardon for her from Couthon, for whom my family had done favors in the past. I came back to Quimper with the signed order, but in spite of my best efforts, I arrived too late!"

"Too late?"

"My poor sister's head," went on the chevalier, sobbing, "had just rolled onto the scaffold as I watched."

"Oh!" said the count, taking the young man's hands.

"Why did I not fall dead? Why did I not cry out? Why did I not ask for the return of the one whose life I held in my hands? I can't tell you, but I thank heaven for the inspiration it gave me. All the unfortunate victims were crowded together there. The executioners didn't even know who they were. And just as Mademoiselle de Chanteleine was going up, fainting, on the executioner's arm, I stepped forward, made a superhuman effort, and said, 'Pardon! Pardon! This is my sister.' They had to release her to me, and I brought her to this good woman's home. That is why you saw me praying this evening on the grave of one who is no longer with us."

The count had risen to his feet.

"My son!" he said to the chevalier, kneeling before him.

Kernan, prostrate on the floor, bathed the young man's feet with his tears.

Chapter VIII

FLIGHT

It is not hard to imagine the night that the count spent close to his daughter, who had been saved from the jaws of death. Although he felt more keenly the loss of the countess, and although he talked to Marie about her poor, saintly, martyred mother, all those sorrows were mingled with an immense joy. What prayers for forgiveness he offered to heaven for his dead wife, and prayers of gratitude for his living daughter and her rescuer!

"Chevalier," said Kernan to the young man, "I will be your faithful dog. My last drop of blood would not repay you for what you have done."

The poor fellow! It seemed as if all that joy must have been hard for him to bear, for his sister had paid for it with her life.

In the morning, Kernan turned his thoughts to the most urgent matter. Since they could not stay in that house without putting the old lady's life in danger, they decided to leave. For the time being, Kernan abandoned his plan to take revenge on Karval. At the moment, the safety of his niece Marie was all-important.

They discussed what to do next.

"My lord," said the Chevalier de Trégolan, "I had already made arrangements to place my poor sister in a fisherman's hut, in the village of Douarnenez, where she would be safe. Do you want to go there and wait for better days, or for an opportunity to leave France?"

The count looked at Kernan.

"Let's go to Douarnenez," he said. "It's good advice, and if we can't find a ship, we'll try to hide so well that no one will suspect we're there."

"I advise you to leave this very morning," said the chevalier. "There is not a moment to lose, and we have to provide for Mademoiselle de Chanteleine's safety as soon as possible."

"But at Douarnenez," asked the count, "will we find food without arousing suspicion?"

"Yes. I have an old family servant there who works as a fisherman, old Locmaillé. He'll welcome us with open arms, and we can live in his house until an opportunity comes up for us to leave France."

"No sooner said than done," replied Kernan. "Let's be on our way as soon as we can. Douarnenez is only five leagues away. We can be there by evening."

The count approved the plan. He was eager to give his daughter a little of the peace and quiet that the poor girl so badly needed. But seeing how weak she was, he was afraid she might not be able to make such a tiring journey. The scene on the scaffold sometimes came back to Marie's mind so vividly that she seemed to be on the point of fainting. She trembled at the slightest noise. She knew that her executioners were still close by. However, her father's caresses, and those of Kernan, helped to restore her strength, and she declared herself ready to face anything in order to leave that city, which had such terrifying memories for her.

The next step was to find her some suitable clothes.

The old lady was sent for, and the count expressed his gratitude to her in the most glowing terms. The good woman was able to provide peasant clothing. The young lady, alone in her room with her benevolent hostess, put it on. With her red woolen stockings, worn thin by frequent laundering, her striped woolen skirt, and the apron of coarse cloth surrounding her entire body, no one would have recognized Marie de Chanteleine.

Marie was a young woman of seventeen. She bore a close resemblance to the count, with her soft blue eyes, now red with tears, and her charming mouth, which was doing its best to smile. She had suffered cruelly during her imprisonment, but a keen observer would have recognized her true beauty. What was left of her blond hair, cropped short by the executioner, was easily concealed under the traditional Breton headdress that she wore. The upper part of her apron covered her bodice, to which it was attached by large pins. Her white hands were rubbed with earth to give them a less suspicious color. Thus attired, she would have been unrecognizable to everyone, even to Karval, her deadliest enemy.

In half an hour she was dressed and ready to leave. The town clock was striking seven in the morning. It was barely daylight, and the fugitives, after bidding a fond farewell to the old lady, left the city without being noticed.

First they had to get to the Audierne highway leading to Douarnenez. Kernan was perfectly familiar with the region, and led the little group along roundabout roads that were longer but safer. They could not walk quickly, since Marie was barely dragging herself along, leaning sometimes on her father's arm and sometimes on Kernan's. She was clearly making a great effort to hold herself up. The pure open air, of which she had been deprived during her painful incarceration, and with which she was now filling her lungs, made her somewhat dizzy, as if she were intoxicated by good wine.

After walking for two hours, she was forced to stop and ask for a few moments' rest. The fugitives came to a halt.

"We won't get there today," said Kernan.

"No," agreed the young man. "We'll have to ask for shelter in a house somewhere."

"Every house looks suspicious to me," said the Breton. "If the worst comes to the worst, I'd rather rest for a few hours in a thicket along the way."

"Let's go on, friends," said Marie after a quarter hour's pause. "I can still take a few steps. When I can't go any farther, I'll let you know."

They went on their way again. It had stopped snowing, but it was still cold. Kernan took off his goatskin jacket and put it around the young woman's shoulders.

By eleven o'clock the travelers had covered barely two leagues. They had not yet reached the village of Plonéis. The countryside seemed deserted; there was not even a thatched cottage to be seen. The ground was disappearing under a vast white blanket. Marie could not take another step, and Kernan had to pick her up and carry her. But walking had not kept the poor girl warm, and she lay like ice in the

Breton's arms. The count and the chevalier took off their jackets and wrapped her feet as best they could.

In the evening, after following the highway, they finally managed, with great difficulty, to get to the village of Kermengy. Douarnenez was still a league and a half away , but it was now so cold that they were obliged to stop. Marie was beginning to faint.

"She can't go on any farther," said Kernan. "She needs a few hours' rest."

The count was sitting on the edge of the road, holding his daughter in his arms and trying vainly to warm her with his kisses.

"What can we do? What can we do?" said Kernan. "I don't want to ask for shelter from people who might betray us."

"What!" cried the count in desperation. "Is there not one charitable soul in this country who will take us in?"

"Alas, no," replied the chevalier. "To appeal to the peasants would be to court certain death. The Blue soldiers deal cruelly with people who shelter outlaws. They cut off their ears and send them to the scaffold on the slightest suspicion."

"Monsieur de Trégolan is right," said Kernan. "We would be risking not only our own lives, but this young lady's life as well."

"Kernan," said the count, "all I know is that my daughter can't spend the night in the open. She would die of cold."

"All right," said the chevalier, "I'll go up to the houses in the village and see whether the Terror has destroyed all hospitable feeling among the Breton peasants."

"Go on, then, Monsieur de Trégolan," said the count, clasping his hands together, "and save my daughter's life once more."

The chevalier hurried towards the village. Night had fallen. After walking for a quarter of an hour, the young man reached the first houses, which were all closed and silent. The doors and windows seemed to be so carefully sealed that the smallest ray of light could not get through to the outside.

"People hide here just as they do everywhere," the young man said to himself.

He knocked on several doors and called. There was no answer, but he could tell, by the few plumes of smoke rising into the darkness, that there must be someone living in those houses. He pounded again on the doors and windows. He shouted. No one answered.

But the chevalier did not lose heart. With the thought of the dying young woman always before his eyes, he went to all the houses, knocking from door to door. When he encountered the same silence everywhere, he realized that not one of the inhabitants of that village, accustomed, no doubt, to fear a visit from the Blues, would open the door to him. Those struck by the Terror were made hard and cruel.

After his vain attempt, there was nothing Henry de Trégolan could do but rejoin his companions. Back he went in despair and soon found the count and Marie just as he had left them. The father, sitting on the edge of a ditch, was still trying to warm his daughter in his arms, but in spite of his efforts he felt her becoming colder and colder. Just as the young man arrived, the count, frightened by Marie's lack of movement, looked at her and realized that she was unconscious.

"Good lord! he exclaimed.

"That village is a graveyard," said the chevalier.

"All right, then," said Kernan. "Let's go across the road, into the Nevet forest. We'll spend the night behind the trunk of an oak tree and make a fire of dry wood."

"We have no choice," replied the young man. "Let's go."

Kernan outlined his plan to the count, picked up the young woman again, and crossed the Audierne road, followed by his two companions. A few minutes later they entered the thicket, where the dry branches cracked under their feet. Henry went ahead to clear the way.

They had to push on into the deepest part of the woods in order not to be seen. After a quarter of an hour or more, Henry discovered a big hollow oak that could provide shelter for the young woman. She was carefully placed there, and Kernan, striking sparks from his tinderbox, soon had a bright, crackling fire going.

The kindly warmth soon brought Marie back to consciousness. Her first reaction on awakening was one of profound fear, but when she saw that she was surrounded by her loved ones, she smiled weakly and soon dropped off to sleep.

All that night, the count, Kernan, and the young man watched over her. She was well covered and sheltered, and rested peacefully.

Kernan kept his fire going with dead branches. His companions, crouching or lying down, warmed themselves as best they could. Sleeping was out of the question. Neither the count nor the chevalier could get to sleep under those conditions. They talked for part of the night.

The chevalier told the Count of Chanteleine his family's history, and a sad story it was. The Trégolans, originally from Saint-Pol-de-Léon, had almost all perished in the bloody battles that took place at that town in March of 1793. Their father had fallen before the cannons of General Canclaux, who was trying to reestablish the bridge cut off by the insurgents from Kerguiduff, on the Lesneven road. The young man had tried to die beside his father, but the Republican bullets would have none of him. When he returned to Saint-Pol-de-Léon he found his house in flames and learned that his sister had been dragged off to prison in Quimper. As he mentioned his sister's name, Henry could not hold back his tears, and the count put his arms around him.

Then the count related the story of his own misfortunes, the destruction of his castle and the death of the countess. Their stories shared a common thread of misfortune, and they both wept bitter tears for what the Republic had done to them.

And so the night went by. Kernan kept a careful lookout and sometimes made his way through the neighboring thickets. Fortunately, daylight came, and the fugitives were able to leave their hiding place.

These few hours of rest and sleep had reinvigorated the young woman, and she felt strong enough to walk. She took her father's arm and they were on their way again by eight o'clock in the morning.

At nine o'clock Kernan, who was guiding his companions, left the Audierne road at the village of Ploaré. Half an hour later, the little group reached the entrance to the village of Douarnenez, and the chevalier took them directly to the old fisherman's house.

Chapter IX

DOUARNENEZ

Douarnenez, in Year II of the Republic, was still a village of no more than twenty fishermen's families. This collection of houses, built of fragments of granite, presented a picturesque view to anyone arriving by sea.

The village, long hidden behind the twists and turns of the coastline, appeared all of a sudden, dominated by the single steeple of a church located on top of a hill.

The village lay along the innermost part of the bay and extended down to the water's edge, where it was washed by the highest waves. The roofs of the houses were covered with big stones, to protect them from the violent northwest winds.

The coast of Brittany, from Concarneau to Brest, is indented by a series of bays of all sizes.

The largest bays are those of Douarnenez and Brest, which have a circumference of up to twenty-five leagues. The Bays of Audierne, Les Trépassés, Camaret, and Dinan are really only coves. The Bay of Douarnenez is the most dangerous of all, and many shipwrecks have given it a sinister reputation.

Its southern part is formed by an almost straight point of land, an inverted pyramid eight leagues long, which juts into the ocean at Point Raz.

Its base is about four leagues wide at Douarnenez, where the parishes of Le Poullan, Beuzec, Cléden, Audierne, Pont-Croix, and Plogoff are situated, as well as several scattered villages.

On the north side of the bay, the coastline describes an immense curve, which ends abruptly at Cape Chèvre, where the magnificent Morgat Caves are to be found. Higher up, one can see the Arrée Mountains, shrouded in mist.

Because the bay is not sufficiently enclosed, it is exposed to all the storms coming from the ocean.

For that reason, the sea is always rough there. The fishermen who venture out in their little boats are often in distress, and may wait for days in front of their safe little harbor without being able to make land.

The village is located at the mouth of a small river, which is dry at low tide. That is where the fishing boats go to take refuge in rough weather, for the pier that covers the little port today did not exist at that time, and the houses along the shore were battered by waves slanting in from the sea.

The end of the little river, in the direction of the village, was called Guet.

On this very point stood the cottage of old Locmaillé. Its side windows offered a view of the entire indentation of the bay, from Cape Chèvre as far as Douarnenez. The little house was barely distinguishable from the surrounding rocks. It was not beautiful, but it was solid and safe.

It consisted of a lower hall, with wet nets and fishing equipment hung up to dry around a large fireplace, and three small rooms upstairs, which offered a view of the fisherman's boat, which was either beached or floating, depending on the tide.

The house was home to old Locmaillé, a man of sixty and a devoted family servant. He was another Kernan, but without his education.

That was where the Count of Chanteleine and his daughter were welcomed. The old man made it clear to them that they were to make themselves at home, and as they entered, they breathed an involuntary sigh of satisfaction. The humble cottage struck them as a place where they could find shelter, or even asylum.

Although the dwelling was small, Henry managed to set aside a room for the young woman, another for the count, and even a little office for him. As was the custom, those rooms were not connected with the lower hall, but were accessed by an outside stone staircase.

The main hall was an ideal room for old Locmaillé and for Kernan, who had decided to become a serious fisherman until something better turned up.

It did not take them long to settle in. A fire of dry vines was soon crackling in Marie's room, and half an hour after arriving in Douarnenez, she was truly at home. For the first time, father and daughter could be alone together. When they withdrew, their privacy was respected.

Meanwhile, Kernan, with Locmaillé's help, prepared a frugal lunch of fresh fish and a few eggs. When the count and his daughter came back down, the fugitives sat down in the lower hall. They ate from bowls, using black wooden cutlery, on a rough table without a table cloth. But at least they were safe in the fisherman's house.

"My friends," said the chevalier, "heaven has protected us by bringing us here. But it will only help us if we help ourselves, so let's talk about our future plans."

"My dear boy," replied the count, "we are relying on you. I place my life and my daughter's life in your hands."

"My lord," said the chevalier, "I think the time of your greatest sorrows is over, and I have high hopes for the future."

"So do I," said Kernan. "You are a worthy young man, Monsieur Henry, and the five of us will have to get through this together. But tell me, won't our arrival in the region seem unusual?"

"Not at all. Locmaillé told anyone who would listen that he was expecting his relatives here in Douarnenez."

"Good," replied the Breton, "but won't people find this addition to the family rather strange?"

"No. The Count of Chanteleine is my uncle and Mademoiselle Marie is my cousin."

"Your sister, Monsieur Henry," said the young woman, "your sister. Do I not have to take the place of the noble young woman who is no longer with us?"

"Mademoiselle!" said Henry, with deep emotion is his voice.

"That may be. That may be," replied Kernan. "And I'll be Locmaillé's cousin, if that's all right with him."

"I'm honored," said the old fisherman.

"All right then. The family will be complete, a fisherman's family. It won't be the first time my master and I have plied that trade. We weren't too bad at it in our youth, and I hope we haven't lost the knack of it."

"All right," said the chevalier, "tomorrow we'll sail around the Bay of Douarnenez. Is the boat ready to sail, Locmaillé?"

"It's all set," replied the old man.

Then the count spoke up. "My friends," he said, "if we must stay in this country, if we have to endure this revolutionary upheaval, if we can't flee any farther from our enemies, I'm unreservedly in favor of your arrangements. But must we give up all hope of leaving France?"

"My lord," replied Henry, "if such a plan had been practicable, believe me, I would have suggested it to you already. I myself have long wanted to escape to England, but I have not found a way of doing it. All I can promise you is that, if the opportunity arises, we won't let it slip by, and perhaps, at a great price, we will be able to make it happen."

"Unfortunately, I haven't much money left."

"And I have nothing to live on but my arms and my boat."

"All right, all right," said Kernan. "We'll see about that later on. But right now, my lord, even if you were ten times as rich, even if we had a good boat at our disposal, I wouldn't advise anyone to set sail on it. We're in the worst months of winter, and the sea is terribly rough outside the bay. The storms would soon drive us onto some point along the coast, where we might find ourselves in serious difficulty. My niece Marie must not be exposed to such danger. In the fine weather, if God has still not taken pity on France, we'll see what can be done. But now, the best thing we can think of is to go fishing—since we are fishermen—and to live peacefully in this region."

"Well spoken, Kernan," said the chevalier.

"Well said, Kernan," added the count, "let's do our best to resign ourselves. Let's not ask for the impossible, but be satisfied with what heaven gives us."

Then the young woman spoke up. "My friends," she said, "my uncle Kernan has spoken and we must listen to him, because his advice is good. He knows very well that I would not flinch before the dangers of the sea. But since he considers it impracticable to make a crossing, we have to think of ourselves as having arrived at our destination, and wait. We are not rich. All right, then, we'll work! For my part, I want to make my small contribution to the community."

"Oh mademoiselle," said the young man quickly, "our work is very hard. You were not brought up like the wives and daughters of our fishermen. You can't expose yourself to such exhausting work. And besides, we'll earn a living for you every day."

"Why should you do that, Monsieur Henry," replied the young woman, "if I can find work that is not beyond my strength? It would be a pleasure and a consolation for me. Could I not, if need be, do some sewing or ironing?"

"Why," exclaimed Kernan, "my niece Marie works like a fairy. I have seen her embroider altar cloths for the church of La Palud of which Saint Anne would have been proud."

"Alas, uncle Kernan," replied Marie sadly, "we are not talking now about altar cloths or church ornaments. But there are other jobs to do, more humble and more lucrative."

"I don't see many," said Henry, who did not want the young woman to engage in manual labor. "I assure you that you will find nothing to do around here."

"Unless it would be to sew heavy shirts for the fishermen, or the Blues in Quimper," said Locmaillé.

"Oh!"

"I accept willingly," exclaimed Marie.

"Mademoiselle!" said the chevalier.

"And why not?" said Kernan. "I assure you my niece will manage very well."

"Yes," said the old man, "at five *sous* apiece."

"That's fine, five *sous* apiece," said Kernan. "So, niece Marie, you will be a linen maid."

"That was the occupation of Mademoiselle de Sapinaud and Mademoiselle de Lézardière after they escaped from Le Mans, and if they did it, so can I."

"Then it's settled. Locmaillé will find work for you."

"Agreed."

"And now, Marie, now, my lord, you must rest for the remainder of the day. I'll go with Monsieur Henry to inspect the boat and tomorrow we'll put out to sea."

With that, Henry and Kernan went out. Locmaillé went off to wander through the village. The young woman stayed with her father and set about organizing the little household.

When the chevalier and Kernan reached Point Guet, they found the boat in perfect condition. It had two tall red sails and had been built to withstand the sea in heavy weather.

A few fishermen who were there mending their nets came over to chat, just to pass the time of day. Kernan answered their questions like a seasoned mariner. He gave his opinion about a little black cloud that looked ominous, but he still made ready to set sail like a man who knew what he was about. And the next day, he put out to sea along with the chevalier, with whom he had developed a close friendship.

The chevalier was indeed a fine and upstanding young man. He had faced courageously the terrible situation that the Revolution was inflicting on people of his age and family background. He was barely twenty-five years old, but those events brought a singular maturity to his mind, in the midst of the atmosphere that was setting France ablaze. Having lost everything, alone and with no family, it seemed only natural that Henry de Trégolan should transfer all his affection and devotion to the count and his daughter. Kernan felt this clearly and could already foresee certain future arrangements that were not displeasing to him. Quite the contrary.

By the superhuman cool-headedness that young Trégolan displayed when he rescued Mademoiselle de Chanteleine, by the courage he showed in his work as a fisherman, Kernan could tell that he was skillful, wise, and determined by nature. He was a man in every sense of the word, that is to say, a solid support, not to be looked down on during that period of social upheaval.

When Kernan liked someone, he truly liked him, and made no secret of it. He often expressed to the count his considered opinion of Henry, and did not wait until Marie was not there to hear it.

A few days after coming to Douarnenez, the count wanted to help his companions in their arduous work, and set out with them. He was still very sad, but fishing provided a happy distraction for his thoughts. Sometimes they had a good day, but five days out of eight the heavy weather prevented the boats from going to sea.

The fish were sold on the spot to shippers, who sent them on to Quimper or to Brest. Some were taken home to be eaten there. In short, the income from fishing and the few *sous* that the young woman earned from her sewing were sufficient to support the little group, who were almost happy in their distress.

Kernan did not want any of the count's money to be spent. Circumstances might become very serious, and it had to be carefully husbanded, in case it became necessary or possible to leave the country.

For his part, if he were ever obliged to escape from Brittany, he would do it; he would not abandon his master. But he would definitely come back to mete out the vengeance that was so important to him. He never spoke about it, however, or made any reference to Karval.

They always made sure that the young woman was not left alone while they were fishing. She always had someone with her, either her father or old Locmaillé.

Besides, the arrival of the newcomers to the region had not surprised anyone. Their presence did not bother anyone in the least. They were accepted as old Locmaillé's relatives, and since they were very helpful, people eventually came to like them. In any case, they had little communication with the outside world, and the noises of the Revolution died out at the door of their cottage.

On January 1, 1794, Henry found the young woman sitting with her father and Kernan, and offered her a small ring as a New Year's present.

"Please accept this, mademoiselle," he said in a voice filled with emotion. "This ring was my sister's."

"Ah! Monsieur Henry," murmured Marie.

She stopped, looked at her father and Kernan, and fell into their arms, weeping profusely. Then she turned back to the chevalier.

"Henry," she said, timidly offering him her cheek, "I have no other present to give you."

The young man brushed his lips gently against Marie's tender cheek, and felt his heart beating wildly in his bosom.

Kernan smiled, and the count involuntarily put together in his mind the names of Henry de Trégolan and Marie de Chanteleine.

Chapter X

TRISTAN ISLAND

The month of January went by uneventfully, and Locmaillé's guests gradually regained their confidence. Trégolan felt more strongly attracted to the young woman with every passing day. Since Marie was under an obligation to him, however, he took as much care to conceal his love as a less tactful person might have taken to display it. No one suspected it, except, perhaps, for Kernan, who had sharp eyes and said to himself, "It will happen, and it's the best thing that could possibly happen."

Douarnenez was a quiet village, and its tranquility was disturbed only once, as we shall see.

On the other side of the river, opposite Locmaillé's house, barely an eighth of a league away, there was an island very close to the shore. It consisted of a single large, barren rock. During the night, a light at the rock's summit marked the entrance to the port. It was called Tristan Island, and it well deserved that name.* Kernan had noticed that the fishermen seemed to regard it with horror. They were very careful not to go near it. Some even shook their fists at it as they went by. Others crossed themselves, and their wives threatened naughty children with "the cursed island."

One might have thought it was the site of a leper colony. It was truly a forbidden place and people were afraid of it.

Sometimes the fishermen said, "The wind is blowing off Tristan Island. The sea will be rough, and some of us will not get home."

---

* "Triste" is the French equivalent of "sad" in English.

That fear was clearly not justified, but the place was still associated with danger and bad luck. And yet it was inhabited. From time to time, a man dressed in black could be seen wandering over the rocks. The people of Douarnenez would point their fingers at him and cry out, "There he is! There he is!"

Often the cries would be accompanied by threats.

The fishermen would repeat angrily, "Kill him! Kill him!"

Then the man in black would go back into a tumbledown hut built at the top of the little island.

This incident occurred several times. Kernan drew the count's attention to it and they asked Locmaillé about it.

"Ah!" he said. "You saw him, then?"

"Yes," replied the count. "Can you tell me, my friend, who this unfortunate person is, who seems to be an outcast from human society?"

"He's the demon!" replied the fisherman in a threatening tone of voice.

"What demon?" asked Kernan.

"Yvenat, the renegade priest."

"What Yvenat? What renegade priest?"

"It's better not to talk about it," was the reply.

That was all they could get from the stubborn old man. But one evening in early February the question came up again as the result of a comment made by Locmaillé himself. The little company had all gathered together in front of the blazing fire in the lower hall. The weather was frightful; wind and rain whistled outside. The hinges of the door and shutters creaked piteously. Great gusts of air came down the wide flue, driving flame and smoke into the room.

Everyone was deep in thought, listening to the storm raging outside, when the old man said, as if he were talking to himself, "This is good weather and a good night for the renegade priest. We couldn't pick a better one."

"Ah! You're talking about that Yvenat," said Henry.

"About the demon, yes. But soon, even if we still talk about him, at least we won't see him any more."

"What do you mean?"

"I know what I'm talking about."

And the old man returned to his thoughts, still listening for some sound he was expecting to hear.

"Henry," said the count, "you seem to know the story of this unfortunate man. Could you tell us who this Yvenat is, this demon?"

"Yes, Monsieur Henry," said the young woman, "I've heard of him, I've even seen the poor fellow on Tristan Island, but I couldn't find out anything more about him."

"This Yvenat, miss," replied Trégolan, "is a constitutional priest, who has sworn allegiance to the Republic . He's a renegade, as people say, and now that the Municipality of Quimper has appointed him to their parish, the only way he can escape the fury of his parishioners is to take refuge on that island."

"Ah!" exclaimed the count. "He's a priest who supports the Revolution, one of those priests who subscribe to the Civil Constitution of the Clergy."

"Right you are, my lord," replied Trégolan. "As soon as the soldiers who brought him here had left, you see what happened to the poor devil. He had to escape by boat and take refuge at the top of that island, where he lives on shellfish."

"And why doesn't he run away?" asked Kernan.

"Boats are not allowed to go near the island, and eventually the poor man will die."

"It won't be long now," murmured Locmaillé.

"The poor devil!" said the count with a deep sigh. "So that's all the good it did him to go along with the Civil Constitution. He didn't realize what a sublime role a priest plays during these times of upheaval and terror."

"Yes," said Trégolan, "it is a noble mission."

"It is indeed," continued the count enthusiastically, "even nobler than the role of the Vendéans and the Bretons who have taken up arms in defense of the holy cause. I have had a close look at those ministers of heaven. I have seen them blessing and absolving an entire army as it knelt before going into battle. I have seen them celebrating mass on a small, isolated hill, with a wooden cross, earthenware vessels, and vestments of coarse cloth. And then I have seen them rushing into the thick of battle, crucifix in hand, helping, comforting, absolving the wounded, even in the face of Republican cannon fire. I thought they were more to be envied there than they were before, in all the pomp of religious ceremonies."

As he spoke, the count seemed to be animated by the sacred fire of the martyrs. His face shone with Catholic fervor. It was clear that he had an unshakable conviction, which would have made him a determined confessor of the faith.

"After all," he added, "during these terrible and trying times, if I had not been a husband and father, I would have liked to be a priest."

Everyone looked at the count's face. It was glowing.

Just then, a dull sound was heard above the howling of the storm. Human threats were mingled with the threat of the elements. It was still an indistinct noise, but no doubt Locmaillé knew what it was all about, for he stood up and said, "Good! There they are! There they are!"

"What's going on?" asked Kernan.

He went over to the door. It was only slightly ajar, but the wind caught it with such force that the sturdy Breton had all he could do to close it again.

But even this brief glimpse outdoors enabled him to see, along the shoreline, lighted torches waving about in the wind. Terrible cries rang out during the short lulls in the storm. There were sinister events afoot for that night.

Formerly, before the Revolution, priests had been held in great veneration throughout the whole of Brittany. They had not engaged in the excesses and abuses that had marked the clergy in the more highly developed provinces. In that corner of France they were kind, humble, and helpful, and came, so to speak, from the best elements of the population. There were a great many of them, and no one ever dreamed of complaining about them. There were up to five priests in each parish, and sometimes as many as twelve. In the department of Finistère alone, there were more than fifteen hundred clergy. The curés, or, as they were called in Brittany, the rectors, enjoyed considerable power, but used it wisely. They appointed their priests, registered birth, marriage, and death certificates, contracts, and wills. They almost all had tenure in their posts, and had numerous young clerks working under them, who lived among the peasants, instructing them in their religious duties and teaching them hymns.

When the time came to take the oath, and the Civil Constitution of the Clergy came into effect, all the priests of France were expected to adhere to it. But the French clergy was divided into two groups, those who took the oath and those who did not. The latter were the most numerous. They refused to swear and had to choose between prison and exile. A sum of thirty-two *livres* was paid to anyone who would bring recalcitrant priests to the district authorities. Finally, on August 26, 1792, a law was passed providing for their mass deportation.

For a fairly long time, the refractory priests were able to evade denunciation and prosecution by their enemies, but the hatred did not abate. Soon they were all captured and deported or massacred, and whole departments were deprived of their old friends.

That is what happened in Finistère, where the clergy were relentlessly hunted down. The priests soon disappeared, and no sacraments were celebrated whatsoever.

Then the Municipalities introduced constitutional priests. The parishioners refused to accept them. Fighting and battles broke out in several places, as the peasants drove away the priests who had taken the oath. In some instances, the takeover of a parish led to bloodshed.

On December 23, 1792, the national guards from Quimper came to install the priest Yvenat at Douarnenez. He was not a bad man—far from it. Before the unfortunate business of the oath, he had always carried out his priestly functions with dignity. He was certainly an honest man, whose conscience did not forbid him to recognize a constitution that had, after all, been signed by Louis XVI. Although he had taken the oath, he would certainly have carried out his ministry with dignity.

But he had taken the oath, and the peasants wanted nothing to do with him. They did not think rationally about the matter, but were guided by their emotions. Right from the start, Father Yvenat began to have problems. He could not find anyone to work for him at the presbytery. His bell ropes were cut, so that he could not ring out the religious offices. Children were unwilling to serve at mass, and their parents would not have allowed them to. They preferred to do without it. Eventually he ran out of wine for the sacrament, and there was not an innkeeper who would have dared to sell him any. Yvenat's work and patience were in vain. He got nothing in return. No one spoke to him, except to insult him, and insult soon led to injury. Then superstition entered into it. He was seen as an evil spirit, a demon. He was accused of causing storms and blamed for shipwrecks. There were riots and finally public anger grew to the point where the priest had to move out of the presbytery. He took refuge on Tristan Island, where the fishermen left him dying of starvation. He had been living on that isolated rock for more than a month, living on wild vegetables and fishing when he could. Charity did not seem to be meant for him.

But the peasants' patience was coming to an end and their anger returned with the calamities that were visited on them every day. The Bretons who escaped the Republican bullets during the war in the Vendée returned to their homes exhausted, wounded, barely dragging themselves along. Hardship increased and the land was threatened with famine. In a superstitious region, so much suffering could only have been attributed to the demon. After the poor devil had been left to vegetate on a bare rock, hatred focused on him again. There was no telling how far those rough peasants would carry it. Eventually the explosion came, announced by the shouts that Kernan had just heard.

Henry de Trégolan had given his companions all the details about Yvenat's life, and when Kernan told him what he had seen through the half-open door, he realized that the threats were aimed at the priest and his life was in danger.

It never occurred to brave people like the count and his friends that one man, whatever his faults, should be abandoned to the fury of an aroused populace. With one accord, they stood up.

"Father," exclaimed Marie, "where are you going?"

"To prevent a crime," replied the count.

"Stay here, my lord," said Kernan. "Monsieur de Trégolan and I will go. My niece Marie can't be left alone. Come on, Monsieur Henry, come with me."

"I'm with you," replied the young man, as he hastily shook the count's hand.

Then he and Kernan rushed out, while old Locmaillé shook his head disapprovingly.

Henry and Kernan hurried towards the beach, in the direction of the loudest shouts that reached them. There, the people of Douarnenez, together with people from Pont-Croix, Le Poullan, and Crozon, were walking along through the storm, accompanied by women and children, shaking their blazing pine torches. They crossed the Guet River by boat and reached a point on the other side directly opposite Tristan Island.

Kernan and Henry had managed to place themselves in the front ranks of the crowd. It would have been madness to try to hold the mob back; it would be wiser to try to take their victim away from them.

At that point the most hot-headed of the fishermen leaped into boats, about twenty of them, and rowed towards the island.

The crowd who stayed behind on the beach was howling. Shouts of hate rang out.

"Kill him! Kill the false priest!"

"Smash his head in with a club!"

"Give the demon a good crack with a pole!"

The unfortunate priest, awakened by those cries of rage, had come out of his hut. He could be seen running in terror across the island, from which there was no escape. He was sure he would die a frightful death. He was running back and forth, his hair flying, dressed in an old cassock that had been torn on the sharp rocks.

Soon the attackers landed on the island and headed towards the demon, shaking their torches as they ran. Kernan was first in line, as if he were the most eager for revenge.

The frantic Yvenat had fled towards the sea, but eventually, with his back to a rock, he no longer had any means of escape. He was sure to die. Cries rang out all around him, and all the anguish of his final hour was depicted on his white face.

Two or three fishermen were running towards him with upraised sticks, but Kernan got there first, picked him up in his arms, and leaped into the dark, foaming water.

"Kernan!" shouted the chevalier.

"Kill him! Kill him!" cried the attackers, leaning out over the abyss. "Drown him like a dog."

But Kernan, invisible in the darkness, came back to the surface with Yvenat, who could not swim. He held him up, and when the priest regained consciousness, he said, "Keep a tight hold on me."

"Have mercy!" cried the poor devil.

"I'm going to save you."

"You!"

"Yes. Let's get to some spot on the shore. Don't be afraid. I'll hold you up."

The priest did not understand this unexpected rescue. All he knew was that his life could be saved. He clutched the powerful Breton, who was swimming strongly, while death threats rang out in the darkness.

After half an hour, Kernan and the priest reached the shore, well away from the island. The priest was exhausted.

"Can you walk?" the Breton asked.

"Yes, yes!" said Yvenat, making a supreme effort.

"Well then, head across the fields and stay away from the houses. You've got all night ahead of you. By morning you'd better be well on your way to Brest or Quimper."

"But who are you?" asked the priest, with a note of gratitude in his voice.

"An enemy," replied Kernan. "Now go, and may heaven guide you, if it still has pity on you."

Yvenat wanted the shake his rescuer's hand, but Kernan had already left. Dragging himself towards the vacant fields, the priest disappeared into the night.

Kernan was on his way back to the shore when he met the crowd of fishermen.

A hundred hate-filled voices shouted at him, "The demon! Where's the demon?"

"He's dead," was the reply.

Despite the profound silence that followed those words, no one heard Kernan whisper in Trégolan's ear, "He's saved, Monsieur Henry. That was a good deed, and I'll do penance for it."

Chapter XI

A Few Days of Happiness

After that terrible evening, during which a city's entire populace had unleashed its fury against one man, the town of Douarnenez resumed its usual calm, and the fishermen, it must be added, returned to their normal work with more confidence. Now that the demon was dead, they did not think they had to worry about reprisals from the Republicans, who knew nothing about the matter. Such was not the case with the count and his friends. They were afraid that Yvenat's first act on regaining his liberty would be a formal denunciation against the inhabitants of Douarnenez, and that they could expect a visit, sooner or later, from the departmental national guards and the fanatics from the cities.

That would put the count and his daughter in grave danger.

For a few days they lived in a state of mortal fear. Kernan even made preparations for a quick departure, in case that should become necessary. Finally, a week after the aforementioned events, since there was nothing to substantiate the fear of an invasion by the Republicans, the count began to feel reassured.

As for Yvenat, either he had not been able to get to the towns and had fallen into the hands of his parishioners again, or he did not want to take revenge on his enemies and had decided to disappear.

There was a third possibility: that the town councils and the delegates of the Committee of Public safety were too busy with the war in the Vendée, which they had to finish, and with the incipient revolt of the *Chouans,* and had no time for taking vengeance on Father Yvenat.

Whatever the reason, calm continued to prevail in the region. The count's confidence gradually returned and he went back to his usual concerns. It was obvious that his ordeals had aged him prematurely. Kernan was sometimes frightened by this. It seemed to him, in fact, that his master was obsessed by a grand idea, to which he himself was not a party. This was a great sorrow for the faithful Breton, accustomed as he was to sharing all the count's thoughts, but he respected his master's silence.

Marie had also noticed that her father was withdrawing into himself more and more. Every time she went into his room, she found him kneeling fervently in prayer, and she would come back in a highly emotional state, feeling that she was caught by an indefinable worry. When she confided this to Kernan, he reassured her as best he could, although he was not reassured himself.

The days went by, however, with little change in the daily routine. The fishing was not going well, and Locmaillé's guests were reduced to eating their catch more often than selling it. The winter had been very severe. Marie was working at her heavy shirts, and her feeble fingers did their best at that thankless task. Trégolan often helped her with the big hems that she was not strong enough to sew, and when he was not plying the fisherman's trade, he sat at her side, gallantly working as a seamstress. At that time there were many upper-class émigrés who had to earn their living by working with their hands. It was not demeaning; quite the contrary. Henry often made clumsy mistakes, much to the young woman's amusement. However, with or without help, she scarcely earned more than five or six *sous* a day.

During those few hours of work, Henry had recounted the story of his life and that of the poor sister whom he loved so much. Marie's heart went out to the young man, and she gently consoled him.

"Monsieur Henry," she would say, "can I not be your sister? Can I not take the place of that holy martyr who gave her life to save mine?"

And the chevalier would reply, "Yes, you are my sister. You are lovely and kind, as she was. You have her heart and her eyes. I can see her whole soul in you. Yes, you are my sister, my beloved sister."

Then he would stop, and often he would hurry away, to avoid saying anything more, for he felt overwhelmed by another emotion, stronger than brotherly love.

Although the young woman did not realize what was going on in his soul, she also felt an unfamiliar emotion creeping into her own heart, but she took it to be the unbounded gratitude she felt for her rescuer.

The secret of such sentiments, however, cannot remain within generous souls forever without breaking out into the open. One who truly loves is often overwhelmed by his love. He must speak, and since Henry had taken the greatest care not to reveal his true feelings to the young woman, he turned to Kernan as his trusted confidant.

The Breton had seen everything, but he held back.

At first, Henry spoke very evasively.

"If the count were not there for his daughter," he said one day, "what would become of her? Would she not be in a very dire situation as an orphan? How could the poor fugitive escape from her enemies?"

"I'd be there," replied Kernan with a smile.

"Of course you would," Henry went on. "Of course you would. But Kernan, my good friend, who knows where fate may lead you? Perhaps the count might call on you to serve in the Catholic Army. Who would protect Marie then?"

Kernan could very well have answered that he and the count would not both abandon Mademoiselle de Chanteleine, but he pretended to accept the chevalier's argument as irrefutable.

"Yes," he said, "who would protect her then? Ah, Monsieur Henry, she would need a stout heart to love her and a husband's arm to defend her. But who would dare take responsibility for that young woman, a fugitive with no fortune?"

"One would not have to be very bold to do that," replied Henry quickly, "knowing her as we do. Marie has been through some terrible ordeals, and she will make a worthy wife, just the wife that an honest man needs to help him get through these revolutionary times."

"You're right, Monsieur Henry," said Kernan, "If people knew her. But they don't, and it seems hardly likely that we will ever find the right husband for my niece in this village of Douarnenez."

The Breton's object in speaking like that was to get the young man to open up more clearly, but his reply produced exactly the opposite effect. The chevalier thought he detected outright disapproval in those words. He said nothing about it that day, much to Kernan's chagrin.

February went by. During the week, they all worked their hardest. On Sunday the count read the divine service in the lower hall, and the pious souls participated with a truly Catholic fervor. They prayed to

heaven on behalf of their martyrs, and, like true Christians, they also (except for Kernan) prayed for their enemies. The Breton was the sole exception. He was not so Christian as to overlook abuses, and every evening, after his prayer, he swore an oath of vengeance.

Then, if the weather was fine, Kernan would suggest a walk along the coast. As a rule, the count stayed home, while Henry, Kernan, and Marie went off among the rocks. They climbed the hill on which the village of Douarnenez sits. They went up the main road towards the church that overlooks the bay. From there they looked out as far as the eye could see over that arm of the sea, open at the horizon, that has its storms and disasters, just as the ocean has. What a magnificent spectacle the bay is when its water is lashed in a fury. Sometimes they would see a boat coming in late, its sail reefed in, struggling with the waves, sometimes disappearing, and often being blown off course, away from the port. From there the eye continued to Point Raz, that long promontory jutting out into the sea.

Henry, who was very familiar with the region, pointed out these beautiful sights to his companion. He was her teacher, and named all the church steeples for her: Le Poullan, Beuzec, Pont-Croix, Plogoff, each one indicating a deserted parish.

Then their walks continued as far as Sainte-Anne-la-Palud. They walked around the bay and saw in the distance the Arrée range, crumpled on top of each other, like weary mountains that seemed to be lying down in the open countryside.

Another day, the hikers courageously covered the four leagues that took them to Point Raz, where they could hear the roaring of the ocean. The undertow there produced wonderful and terrible effects on the rocks of the little bay with the sinister name: Bay of Trépassés.* The spectacle of the angry water made a deep impression on the young woman. She clung to the chevalier's arm when sheets of foam lifted by the wind fell back in noisy cataracts.

Henry used to tell some old legends, the most famous of which was that of King Canute's daughter, who gave the devil the keys to an immense, bottomless pit. At that time there were vast plains where the bay now lies, but when the gates of the pit were carelessly opened, the water burst out, drowning the towns, the inhabitants, the flocks, the entire fertile region, and forming the arm of the sea that has been known ever since as the Bay of Douarnenez.

"A strange time that was, when people believed such things," said Henry.

"Is our miserable century any better?" was Kernan's response.

"Yes, it is, Kernan," continued the young man, "because periods of ignorance and superstition are always appalling. Nothing good can come out of them. But when God finally takes pity on France, who knows whether humanity may not have derived some benefit, which we cannot foresee, from these terrible excesses? Heaven works in mysterious ways, and evil always contains a germ of good."

* "Trépassés" is the French equivalent of "deceased" in English.

Chatting in this way, and building up a supply of hope for the future, they returned quietly home, their appetites whetted by the long walk. These were truly happy days for the little group. Had it not been for the count's profound depression, the poor fugitives would have asked for nothing better than to have their happiness continue.

However, Henry had not resumed his talk with Kernan, although he had often caught the Breton looking at him and Marie with a sly smile.

But the naïve and simple Marie, without meaning any harm, spoke quite openly to her uncle about the Chevalier de Trégolan, even without his knowledge, with genuine enthusiasm.

"He's really an excellent man," she would say, "a true gentleman at heart. I could not wish to have anyone else as my brother."

Kernan let her talk.

"Sometimes," Marie would go on, "I wonder whether we are not taking advantage of his generosity. Poor Monsieur Henry! He works for us, and goes to so much trouble. We will never be able to repay him for his efforts."

Kernan made no reply.

"And besides that," continued the young woman, who no doubt assumed that the Breton was answering all her questions in the affirmative, "besides that, he is not a fugitive. He has protectors, since he was able to get a pardon for his sister in Paris. And yet he stays in this region, and in this little cottage. He has taken on a rough occupation, at the risk of his life. And for whom does he do that? For us! Heaven will have to reward him some day, because we will be powerless to do so."

Kernan still said nothing, but he smiled, thinking that the reward was not far off.

"After all," said Marie, "don't you think he's a worthy young man?"

"Yes indeed," replied Kernan. "Your father would not want anyone else for a son, and as for me, niece Marie, I would not want any other nephew."

That was the only hint the Breton allowed himself to offer, but he did not know whether it had been understood or not. It is likely, however, that in her conversations with the chevalier, Marie reported Kernan's opinion of him. Several days later, in fact, when Henry was out fishing with Kernan, he openly confessed his feelings, blushing and dropping his net.

"You must speak to her father," was the Breton's only reply.

"Right away?" exclaimed the chevalier, terrified at such haste,

"When we get back."

"But…" said the young man.

"Come about into the wind or we'll capsize."

And that was all. Henry straightened the tiller, but he held it so awkwardly that Kernan was obliged to take his place at the helm.

This incident took place on March 20. For several days before, the count had seemed more worried than usual. Several times, he had taken his daughter in his arms and held her to him without saying a word. When Kernan came back from fishing (a lover's fishing expedition, as it were, and not a very successful one) he spoke first to Marie.

"Where's your father?" he asked.

"My father has gone out," replied the young woman.

"Well!" said Kernan, "that's strange. He doesn't make a habit of doing that."

"Didn't he say anything to you, mademoiselle?" asked Henry.

"No. I offered to go with him, but he just gave me an affectionate kiss and left."

"Well, let's wait until he gets back, Monsieur Henry," said Kernan.

"Did you have something to say to him?" asked the young woman,

"Yes, mademoiselle," Henry stammered.

"Yes," added Kernan, "but it was nothing—nothing important. Let's wait."

They waited. Suppertime came, and the count was not back. They waited patiently, but soon they began to worry. Old Locmaillé had seen the count heading towards the road to Châteaulin. He was walking quickly, with a stick in his hand, like someone on a journey.

"What can that mean?" exclaimed Marie.

"What? He left without telling us!"

Henry hurried to the staircase and went up to the count's room. He soon came back down, holding a letter, which he handed to Marie. It contained only these words:

> *My daughter, I am leaving for a few days. Let Kernan look*
> *after you. Pray for your father.*
>
> *– The Count of Chanteleine*

Chapter XII

The Departure

It is not hard to understand the effect that the reading of those few words had on their hearers. Marie burst out sobbing in spite of herself, and only with the greatest difficulty was Henry able to comfort her.

Where had the Count of Chanteleine gone? Why this sudden departure? Why this secret, which his trusty Kernan had not been able to penetrate?

"He's gone off to fight! He's gone to rejoin the Whites!" cried Marie.

"And without me!" exclaimed Kernan.

But when he stopped to consider that Marie was alone in the world, he realized that the count must have delegated to him the responsibility of protecting her.

A discussion ensued about the suggestion that the count had rejoined the remains of the Catholic Army. It was a highly plausible hypothesis.

Indeed, the struggle was still going on, hotter and more stubborn than ever, in spite of all the wars that the Convention had on its hands and in spite of the Terror that reigned in Paris since the execution of the Girondins. Although the members of the government were in open conflict with some deputies of the Convention, and although, several weeks later, Danton would meet his fate, the Committee of Public Safety was remarkably active.

It is well to recognize what some men of opposing parties thought of this committee, which, by the terrible and bloody measures it adopted, saved France when it was caught up in all the horrors of the civil war and threatened by the coalition.

On Saint Helena, Napoleon said, "The Committee of Public Safety was the only government France had during the Revolution."

De Maistre, of the Legitimist Party, had the courage to agree with that view, saying that the émigrés, after handing France over to the kings, would never have been strong enough to get it back from him.

Chateaubriand held the same view of these twelve men: Barère, Billaud-Varenne, Carnot, Collot d'Herbois, Pierre Prieur from the Marne, Robert Lindet, Robespierre the elder, Couthon, Saint-Just, Jeanbon-Saint-André, Prieur-Duvernois from the Côte-d'Or, and Héraut de Séchelles, whose names are, for the most part, held in general abhorrence.

Be that as it may, the Committee, wanting to bring the revolt in the Vendée to an end, embarked on a campaign of the most horrible devastation. Infernal columns of troops, led by Generals Turreau and Grignon, advanced across the country after the defeat at Savenay, pillaging, massacring, and destroying. No one, women, children, or old men, escaped their bloody reprisals.

The prince de Talmont was captured and executed in front of his ancestral castle. D'Elbée, a sick man, was shot in his armchair between two of his relatives. On January 29, 1794, Henri de La Rochejaquelein, after a final victory over the incendiary columns at Nuaillé, approached two Blue soldiers who had been surprised in a field.

"Surrender," he said, "and I will spare your lives."

But one of the scoundrels raised his musket and shot him dead with a bullet to the middle of his forehead.

Meanwhile, the Committee's bloodiest agents were being sent to the provinces. Since October 8, Carrier, at Nantes, had been designing methods that he called "vertical deportation." On January 22, he began using boats equipped with valves, for the benefit of the prisoners taken from the Vendéan army.

But the more they were decimated, the more eager the Royalists were to fight against the Revolution. It was possible, then, that the Count of Chanteleine had joined Charette, who had resumed the campaign after evacuating the Island of Noirmoutier, or Stofflet, who had just succeeded La Rochejaquelein.

The Catholic Army was broken up, and there began a dreadful campaign of guerilla warfare. Stofflet and Charette, both illustrious

Vendéans, defeated the Republican generals. Charette, who had been conquering Republican troops for three months with ten thousand men, defeated and killed General Haxo.

This news traveled all the way to Brittany, and Douarnenez often thrilled to the noise of battle.

If the count was not in the Vendée, he might have joined the counter-revolutionary *Chouan* movement. During the last months of the disastrous year of '93, Jean Chouan had rebelled, taking with him the entire population of Lower Maine and storming his way from the Mayenne to the Morbihan.

Since there was an important role for Chanteleine to play there, why would he not have accepted it? Trégolan and Kernan discussed all the possibilities. And yet, the count's well-kept secret made Kernan hesitate.

"He would not have hidden from us," he said, "if he had returned to the battlefield."

"Who knows?"

"No, there must be something else."

Then one of them would go in search of news, even risking his life to find out what was happening in the Vendée or the Morbihan. Rumors of a battle filled them with despair. Despite all their efforts, however, they could learn nothing.

Marie trembled and prayed for her father. Looking around her, she came to the conclusion that she was almost completely isolated in the world.

Then she began to have moments of despair. Kernan and the chevalier tried to reassure her, but without success.

The days went by and there was still no news of the count. Rumors from the outside world were alarming.

The count had disappeared on March 20. Six days later the Vendéans resumed the offensive with a glorious feat of arms on March 26, when the town of Mortagne was retaken from the Blues. The commander-in-chief at this action was Marigny, Chanteleine's old comrade. After wandering about for three months, he now reappeared as a conqueror.

When Kernan heard this news, he exclaimed, "Our master is there. He is at Mortagne!"

But when the two men and the young woman learned the details of the bloody battle that had taken place, in which the best soldiers of the Whites had been killed, their anxiety knew no bounds, and when, two weeks after the capture of Mortagne, there was still no news, Marie cried out in despair, "My father! My poor father is dead!"

"My dear Marie," replied Trégolan, "calm yourself. No, your father is not dead. We have no proof of that."

But Marie refused to listen to him. "I tell you he's dead!" she said.

"My dear niece," Kernan went on. "It isn't easy to send news in wartime. All things considered, a victory has been won over the Republicans."

"No, Kernan. There is nothing to hope for. My mother died in her castle and my father on the field of battle. I am alone in the world. Alone! Alone!"

Marie was sobbing. This ordeal had crushed her. Her frail nature could not endure so many blows, one after the other. And although she had no proof that her father was dead, she had made up her mind, as so often happens in times of despair, and nothing could shake her conviction on that score.

However, when Marie cried out that she was alone in the world, Kernan felt a large tear roll down his cheek. His heart was bleeding, and he could not refrain from saying, "Marie, my niece, your uncle is still with you."

"Kernan, my good friend," replied the young woman, gripping the Breton's hand.

"You will always have a friend to love you," he continued.

"Two!" exclaimed Trégolan impulsively. "Two, my dear Marie, for I love you!"

"Monsieur Henry!" said Kernan.

"Forgive me, Marie. Forgive me, Kernan, but those words were choking me. No! My beloved is not alone in the world. No! I will be happy to devote my whole life to her."

"Henry!" exclaimed the young woman.

"Yes, I love her. You know that, Kernan. Her father entrusted her to you, and you approve of my love."

"Monsieur Henry, why do you say such things, since…"

"Don't be afraid, Kernan, or you, my dear Marie. If I have spoken like this, it's because I'm going away."

"Going away!" cried Marie.

"Yes, I'm leaving you—the one I love, and from whom I would have liked to take with me some kind word. If I had had to stay, I would have kept this secret locked up in my heart, as I had promised

Kernan. But I'm leaving. For how long? I don't know. And now, will you forgive me for having spoken?"

"But where are you going, Henry?" asked Marie, in a tone of voice that pierced the young man's very soul.

"Where am I going? To Poitou, to the Vendée, to Mortagne, wherever I might meet your father, wherever I might hear news of him, so that I can tell you whether you still have another heart on this earth to love you, besides Kernan's and mine."

"What?" said Kernan. "You want to join the count?"

"Yes, and I'll do it. I'll find him or die in the attempt."

"Henry!" cried the young woman.

"All right then, Monsieur Henry, go," said Kernan, in a voice filled with emotion, "and may heaven protect you. While you're away I'll look after this dear young lady. But be careful. You know that we expect to see you again."

"Don't worry, Kernan. My task is not to get killed out there, but to find the Count of Chanteleine. He can't be so well hidden that I won't be able to find him. His rank in the Royal Army will guarantee that he is not unknown. I'll go to Mortagne, Marie, and I'll bring you news of your father."

"Henry," said the young woman, "you will face many dangers for our sake. May God go with you, and may he reward you."

"When are you leaving?" asked Kernan.

"This evening, after dark. I'll go on horseback or on foot, depending on the circumstances, but I'll get there."

Preparations for Henry's departure were quickly completed. When the time came for him to go, the young woman took the chevalier's hand in both of hers and held it for a long time, unable to speak. Kernan was deeply moved. But Henry found a superhuman strength in the young woman's eyes, and, after a long farewell, he headed for the door.

Just at that moment, the door opened suddenly to reveal a man wearing an overcoat.

It was the count.

"My father!" cried Marie.

"My beloved daughter," replied the count, clasping Marie to his bosom.

"Oh! We were so worried while you were away, father. Monsieur Henry was about to go and find you and bring you back to us."

"Good lad!" said the count, holding out his hand to the chevalier, "You were ready to sacrifice yourself for us again."

"Everything is all right, then," said Kernan. "I definitely believe that fate had a hand in this."

The count, who had not spoken about the reason for his absence, was equally silent about the goal he had achieved. It seemed obvious to the Breton that the journey had something to do with a Royalist plot, a new conspiracy of some kind, but he did not question his master about that.

He considered it his duty, however, to bring the father up to date about what had transpired. He told him of the love to which he had been privy, and how, when Marie was in the depths of despair, the young man had let slip a confession of that love. He had no doubt that the young woman loved him.

"And certainly, no man was ever more worthy of being loved," he added. "After all, my lord, if this marriage were decided on, it could not be celebrated, because there is no priest in the region, and we would have to wait."

The count shook his head and said nothing.

Chapter XIII

The Mysterious Priest

The absence of priests in the department had brought religious observances to a complete halt, a state of affairs that was especially hard on the rural population. And yet, rather than recognize the constitutional priests, people stayed in their homes and shunned the churches. As a result, newborn children were not baptized, the dying did not receive the last rites, and no marriages, either religious or civil, could be performed, since no registry offices had been set up because of the unrest.

During the last half of April, however, a definite change came about in the countryside in the part of Finistère lying within a few leagues of Douarnenez. It was soon evident that a priest had returned to the region to brave the countless dangers and carry out his noble work.

At first this was only whispered about. It would not do to attract the attention of the spies that the Municipalities kept everywhere. But eventually it became clear that a mysterious man was traveling through the region. In darkness, storm, and rain, an unknown man, always alone, was going about the countryside, visiting villages—Pont-Croix, Crozon, Douarnenez, Le Poullan—and his journeys took him not only into the parishes but also into the most isolated homes.

He seemed to know the region perfectly and to be well-informed as to its needs. When a child was born, he would appear. He brought comfort and the last rites to the dying. He was not often seen, for his face was usually covered, but there was no need to see him. The sound of his voice was enough to show that his ministry was one of religious charity.

It was not long before this fact, so little known at first, attracted public attention. Soon it was being talked about in Douarnenez.

"Last night he came to see mother Kerdenan and gave her the last rites," said one.

"The day before yesterday," said another, "he baptized the Brezenelts' baby."

"Let's take advantage of this while he's here," said the others naively, "for he could easily meet with some misfortune."

The people living along the coast (who were pious folk, after all) were glad of the stranger's presence, since he was restoring the moral tone of the region.

There was an old oak tree on the road from Douarnenez to Pont-Croix, where people who wanted the comfort of religion would leave a note or sign of some sort, and the mysterious priest would appear the following night.

Because they were so isolated, Locmaillé's guests were not aware of this new state of affairs at first. They seldom talked with their neighbors and were quite content to stay at home. For at least two months, this holy mission was carried on without their being informed of it or being able to take advantage of it for themselves.

But old Locmaillé found out what was happening and mentioned it to Kernan. The Breton had nothing more urgent to do than to tell his master about it. The count's eyes lit up with satisfaction.

"My word," said Kernan, "that priest must be a brave and devoted man, because it takes devotion and courage to do what he's doing."

"Yes," replied the count, "but for him, doing good is its own reward."

"No doubt, my lord, and I can understand why the people along the coast here are happy to have him in the region. It was hard, you know, to die without making confession."

"Yes," replied the count.

"In my opinion," went on the Breton with deep conviction, "that would have been the saddest thing of all. A new-born child can wait to be baptized, and anyone is entitled to take the place of a priest beside a cradle. Young people can postpone a wedding until happier times. But to die without a confessor at your bedside, that would drive one to despair."

"You are right, my poor fellow."

"But I'm thinking," went on the Breton, "there is something here that will please Monsieur Henry. We owe a great deal to that courageous young man, and fortunately it will be easy for us to show our gratitude

to him. You know, he will be a dependable husband to my niece. By allowing him to save her, heaven was certainly reserving her for him at some future date."

"We must believe that, Kernan," replied the count. "If only that dear child can enjoy the happiness she deserves! After all she has been through, heaven should grant her a happy life from now on. But before you talk to the chevalier about this priest, Kernan, let me see what I can arrange."

Kernan promised to say nothing, but the chevalier soon got wind of what people throughout the region were talking about. He immediately went to tell Kernan about his great discovery, and the Breton could not suppress a smile.

"Let's talk about this at supper this evening," he said, "and you'll see what answer you get."

Henry followed Kernan's advice, and that very evening, taking Marie's hand, he addressed the Count de Chanteleine as "father."

"But this priest," he said, "who will see him?"

"I will," said the count.

Marie fell into his arms.

"That's fine. That's fine," said Kernan. "It will bring us luck. I wouldn't be surprised if this was the end of the matter. Ah! Monsieur Henry, you'll really like him."

"Yes, uncle," said Henry, throwing his arms around the Breton's neck.

Another long month went by, and the count said nothing more about the mysterious priest. Had he seen him? Henry hardly dared inquire. But one evening, the count announced to his children that their marriage would be celebrated in the Morgat Caves on July 13. That meant another three weeks to wait.

There was nothing to do but wait patiently. The time that leads to happiness seems very long, and yet it is the time that goes by most quickly. There were a thousand little things to be done. Kernan wanted Marie to be beautiful in her wedding dress, and he spent a few old *écus* to buy her a ribbon here, a chemisette there. Henry really reduced himself to poverty, which was not difficult. Without saying a word, he went to Châteaulin one day and brought back some beautiful Breton peasant women's clothing.

It should be added that Kernan considered it a point of honor to appear at the ceremony with good, heavy shoes, and even old Locmaillé was determined to have new clogs.

Everything was ready before the appointed day. Henry was still worried about the priest and would have liked to see him. Having heard about the tree trunk, he went there one morning and left a note reminding the mysterious priest about the important date—July 13—and the Morgat Caves.

A few moments later, a rather disreputable-looking man picked up the note and quickly disappeared.

The eve of the great day finally arrived. The last evening was spent in the lower hall. Henry could hardly contain himself for joy. The count talked to his children about life's important duties and how best to carry them out. He spoke fondly to them. Henry and Marie fell to their knees and asked him to bless them.

"Yes," said the count, "may heaven bless you. May it absolve you through my voice. May it protect you for the rest of your lives. Yes, my beloved children, may it bring you a father's blessing."

Then, lifting them to their feet, he kissed them both.

Chapter XIV

THE MORGAT CAVES

Cape Chèvre is the tip of a long point of land formed by the curving north shore of the Bay of Douarnenez, which it partially encloses. The promontory itself marks off a sort of small interior bay, clearly visible from the village, a little to the left.

The famous Morgat Caves are located near the central part, on a magnificent beach. There are several of them. They are accessible at low tide, except for the largest and most beautiful one, which can be entered only when the tide is full.

This is an enormous cave, with depths which the human eye has never beheld, for lack of air to breathe. Torches that are taken there flicker and finally go out. No living creature could survive there. But the entire front part of the cave is spacious, airy, and grandiose in appearance.

That was the spot chosen for the wedding celebration. The rumor soon spread throughout the neighboring parishes that a solemn mass was going to be celebrated there. The effect of this news on a population deprived of religious ceremonies for so long is not hard to understand. Crowds of local people decided to come to the Morgat Caves, especially since the location would protect the faithful from being taken by surprise.

The fishermen, who would have to stay on their boats to hear mass, could easily escape any Blues who tried to surprise them by land. That was the reason behind the priest's decision to hold the ceremony in public.

The day arrived, with a brisk and favorable wind. In the morning a great number of boats, crowded with men, women, children, and old folk, left the port of Douarnenez to cross the bay. It was a magnificent sight, this flotilla setting sail with the fishermen dressed in their finest apparel.

Trégolan's boat was in the lead. Marie was charming in her Breton bridal outfit, looking happy, but still a bit melancholy. Henry was holding her hand. Kernan was at the tiller and old Locmaillé in the bow.

The Count of Chanteleine had left early in the morning, before breakfast. It was essential that everything should be ready and especially that the main character, the priest, should be there.

And so the flotilla sailed along over a calm sea. Sometimes, when the wind freshened, all the sailboats heeled over in unison and straightened up when the gust had passed. The village of Douarnenez was already fading into the distance.

Soon the cave came into view. There was no steeple to mark it and no bell joyfully ringing out a wedding mass, but the piety of the entire populace would transform it into a natural church.

When they arrived in front of the cave, the tide was still not high enough for them to enter. The boats arranged themselves in an orderly fashion and waited.

At last the sea began to flow over the beach, foaming at first over the sand and then more calmly as the tide rose. The boats entered and formed a circle along the granite walls, which were faced with red rocks and took on a shade of carnelian that was a delight to behold.

In the center of the cave stood an isolated rock, a little island only a few feet square, on which an altar had been erected. A few candles were burning in wooden candlesticks and the last wavelets were lapping at the foot of this altar, while the boats rocked gently in the swell.

But Marie kept looking around anxiously.

"Where is my father?" she asked Kernan.

"He's sure to be here soon," he replied.

"Marie, I love you," Henry whispered in the young woman's ear.

Soon, at the back of the cave, a little bell rang out and a boat slowly approached. A child was shaking the bell, a fisherman was sitting in the front, rowing, and at the stern a priest was holding the chalice. When he reached the rock, he got out of the boat, placed the sacred vessel on the altar, and turned to face the assembled guests.

"It's my father!" exclaimed Marie.

"So it is!" said Kernan.

The priest was none other than the Count of Chanteleine. His family were thunderstruck and could not believe their eyes. As they stood there in complete silence, the count began to speak.

"My brothers, my friends," he said, "the one speaking to you is a father. As a widower, he became a priest in order to bring you the comforts of religion. A holy bishop, in hiding near Redon, has given

him the authority to carry out that sacred calling. He has come to give his daughter in marriage to the man who saved her from the scaffold, and he asks you to pray for her."

These words brought a shiver to the crowd. The fishermen all recognized the man who was speaking to them and understood his sublime devotion. Marie was weeping and Kernan could not utter a word.

The count's absence was now explained. The theological studies he had pursued in his youth had enabled him to pass rapidly through the initial stages of the priesthood and in a few days he had been ordained.

Now that he was back with his family, he spent his nights in carrying out his holy ministry. He left the house by the outside staircase, without anyone suspecting that he was gone. The reason he had not revealed the secret of his new existence to his friends and his daughter sooner was that he did not want to frighten them with fears of the dangers to which he was exposing himself.

Taking hold of the engaged couple's boat, the count brought it up to the foot of the rock, and the mass began.

There was something touching about the sight of this widower-priest, this father giving his daughter in marriage. Everyone was overcome by the unusual nature of the situation.

Soon the murmuring of prayer mingled with the murmuring of the waves. The emotion in the count's voice was audible.

The moment of the elevation finally arrived. The little bell rang out, the faithful bowed in deep meditation, and the priest was raising the consecrated host to heaven when shouts were heard outside.

A voice shouted "Fire!" and a frightful volley rang out.

"The Blues! The Blues!" people cried out on all sides.

Every boat attempted to escape from the cave, under fire from a man-o'-war, the *Sans-Culotte,* which had anchored in front of the beach. It had launched its boats and they were heading for the cave, filled with soldiers.

There was total chaos. Wounded people were dying. Some were trying to climb up onto the rocks and reach the open country. Others were drowning in the midst of the smoke. People could not see each other. The Republicans entered the cave. A boat came up to the altar and a man leaped out onto it.

"Aha! Chanteleine, I've got you," he shouted, seizing the priest and handing him over to the soldiers. "Priest and aristocrat, your time is up."

The man was Karval. The note left by Henry had been intercepted by a spy who was keeping an eye on the region. When Karval was told of the incident, he immediately left Brest by ship and came to take the poor people by surprise.

Kernan had caught sight of Karval, but on hearing the count cry out, he pushed the boat away vigorously and took refuge in the darkest part of the cave.

Karval, however, had had time to recognize Marie, much to his surprise, for he thought she was dead. He mounted a search for her everywhere when the smoke had cleared, and Kernan, to escape from his enemies, unhesitatingly took the boat into one of the deep caverns where he was in danger of dying for lack of air.

Karval continued his search, swearing and blaspheming.

"Nothing! Nothing! The girl is getting away from me. Was she not executed, then? How could they have escaped?"

He was brought out of the cave. The fishermen who had been able to reach the shore were running away in all directions. Karval saw nothing and had to be satisfied with having captured the count.

The count had been put on board the warship, which took to the open sea and made for Brest.

Kernan, however, was in a dreadful situation. The young woman was lying at his feet in a faint and Henry felt that he was suffocating. When Karval's boat eventually left the cave, the Breton lost no time in escaping from that deadly hiding-place, and he revived Marie by moistening her pale face.

"She's alive! She's alive!" cried the young man.

"My father!" murmured Marie.

Henry said nothing, while Kernan made an angry, threatening gesture.

"Ah Karval," he said, "I'm going to kill you!"

Leaving Marie in the care of the chevalier, whose marriage to her had not yet been blessed, Kernan plunged into the water and swam across to the shore. Not seeing the Republicans there, he slowly emerged from the water and went up onto the beach, where he found dead bodies and blood. He climbed up onto the rocks and joined a few unfortunate folk who were hiding.

"Well," he asked them, "where are the Blues?"

"There."

They pointed to the warship, which at that moment was rounding Cape Chèvre.

"And the priest?" asked Kernan.

"He's on that ship," replied the fishermen.

Kernan slid down from the top of the bank onto the beach and went back into the cave. Then he dived into the water again and returned to the boat where Marie was lying, barely breathing.

"And the count?" asked Henry.

"He's being taken to Brest."

"All right then," exclaimed Henry. "We have to go to Brest, to rescue him or die in the attempt."

"I agree," replied Kernan. "Besides, we can't go back to Douarnenez. We wouldn't be safe there now. Locmaillé will take the boat back. We'll hide somewhere near Brest and wait."

"But how will we get there?"

"We'll have to go overland to the harbor at Brest."

"But what about Marie?"

"I'll carry her," said Kernan.

"I'll walk," said the young woman, standing up with a superhuman effort. "To Brest! To Brest!"

"Let's wait until dark," said Kernan.

The whole day went by in fear and despair. The poor people had been struck with a thunderbolt in the midst of their happiness.

Kernan brought the boat out on the evening tide. When night had fallen, he reached the beach, shook hands with old Locmaillé, and, supporting Marie, set out across the fields.

In half an hour the fugitives reached the village of Crozon, half a league from the caves. On the way they passed dead bodies that were still warm. They walked on like that for more than an hour.

Where were these poor people going? What were they going to do? What were they hoping for? How could they snatch the count from the brink of death? They had no idea, but they kept going. They went through the villages of Pen-ar-Menez, Lescoat, Laspileau, and finally, after walking for two hours, arrived at Le Fret, which is situated on the roadsted of Brest.

Marie could go no farther, but fortunately, Kernan found a fisherman who was willing to take her across the harbor.

They boarded the boat, and at one o'clock in the morning disembarked, not at Brest, but on the coast leading to Recouvrance, near Le Portzic, right at the door of a shabby inn, where they were able to find a room.

Kernan went out the next day, looking for news. He learned that the warship *Sans-Culotte* had captured an important prize on the coast of Brittany and was now back in Brest.

Back he went to the inn.

"Now, Henry," he said, "I'll leave you with your fiancée. I'm going to town. I want to know what I'm up against."

Kernan left, following the coastline, and entered through Recouvrance. When he arrived at the port of Brest, he crossed it by boat. He then went up to the castle and prowled around it all day.

Brest was in the grip of the most frightful terror. Blood was flowing freely in the public squares, where Jeanbon Saint-André, a member of the Committee of Public Safety, was carrying out unbelievably horrible reprisals.

The Revolutionary Tribunal was working without letup. They even had children operating the guillotine, "to teach them to read what is in the souls of the Republic's enemies."

Madness was mingled with bloody intoxication.

By asking around here and there, Kernan learned that the count had been imprisoned and condemned to death, but his execution was being postponed for a particularly cruel reason.

Karval wanted the young woman to be guillotined before her father's eyes, and he had sworn to capture her at all costs.

"That cannot happen," Kernan said to himself. "There are some things that heaven will not permit."

Be that as it may, Karval, after accepting the congratulations of the clubs and the proconsul, returned to Douarnenez the same day and continued his search.

Kernan went back to Le Portzic in the evening. He told the two young people that the count's execution had been postponed, but without mentioning the reason. He announced his intention of going to Brest every day to see what was happening there. But above all, he advised them not to set foot outdoors.

Marie, meanwhile, was lying down, near death. This last ordeal had been too much for her.

For thirteen days, Kernan left in the morning and returned in the evening without bringing any new information. Most of the fishermen arrested at Morgat had been executed, along with their wives and children. As for the count, only a miracle could save him.

On the evening of the thirteenth day, July 26, Kernan, who had left in the morning as usual, did not return, and Henry spent the night in mortal anxiety.

Chapter XV

The Confession

As it happened, Kernan's return had been delayed by an unexpected meeting. It was nine o'clock in the evening and he was going home in despair. The execution of the former Count of Chanteleine was announced for the following day. Karval, unable to find the young woman, had finally ordered the death sentence to be carried out.

Kernan was determined to use extreme measures to get the count out of the deadly tumbrel that would convey him to the scaffold. But he wanted to see the chevalier and his niece Marie, perhaps for the last time, before deciding on a course of action. He strode along, after spending a long time prowling around the prison.

He had already crossed the port of Brest and was walking up the steep and winding streets of Recouvrance, when he noticed, walking ahead of him, a man whose bearing struck him as unusual. It was not so dark yet that he could be mistaken. Certain details made him think that this man was the one he hated so much. Soon he could have no doubt about it.

"Karval!" he said to himself. "Karval!"

Hatred, anger, the thirst for vengeance, all blinded him for a moment, to the point where he was ready to leap on the scoundrel and kill him on the spot. But he managed to control himself.

"I've got him," he said, "in cold blood!"

Kernan began to follow Karval. He took off his shoes. He fell back a certain distance in order not to be noticed, and, running barefoot when his enemy turned a corner, he picked up his trail again like an Indian on the North American prairie.

Karval entered one of the small, steep side streets, so numerous in that part of the city. It was gradually getting darker and the streets were becoming deserted. Kernan had to get closer to Karval in order not to lose sight of him. The scoundrel had no idea that the Breton was in the city, and would not have recognized him. He soon realized, however, that he was being followed, and lengthened his stride. Kernan, fearing every moment that a door might open up in front of Karval, decided to confront him. He quickened his pace and caught up with him near the town fortifications, where the sentries make their rounds.

Karval backed off quickly and said, in a rather nervous voice, "What do you want with me, citizen?"

Taking hold of his arm, Kernan replied, "I want to denounce someone."

"This is not the time or the place," replied Karval.

"Oh yes it is, for a patriot like you. My business concerns the Republic."

"All right, then, what do you want?"

"You're looking for Citizen Marie de Chanteleine."

"Ah!" said Karval, whose hatred was restoring his confidence,. "Do you know where she is?"

"She's in my power," replied Kernan, "and I can turn her over to you."

"Right away?"

"This very moment."

"And what are you asking in return?" said the scoundrel.

"Nothing. Come with me."

"Wait. The military post on the ramparts is not far from here. I'll go and get a few men and tomorrow, at the latest, Citizen Chanteleine will fall dead before her father's eyes."

Kernan's steely grip tightened so violently on Karval's arm that he cried out in spite of himself. Just then, the light from a street lamp fell on Kernan's face and Karval looked at him. Suddenly, his face lost its composure and he shouted out distinctly, "Kernan! Kernan!"

He wanted to call for help, but his voice failed him. He was trembling. The criminal was the most cowardly of men. And he had good reason to be afraid. Kernan's face was shining, and in his hand he held a broad cutlass, its point pressed against the Republican's chest.

"One word and you're dead," said the Breton in a deep voice. "You're coming with me."

"But what do you want?" stammered the wretch.

"I want to show you Mademoiselle de Chanteleine. Take my arm, and no nonsense. You're in no position to do anything. We're going to walk past houses with people living in them, even past some military posts. You'll still feel this blade pressing against your heart. If you make the least sound, I'll drive it home. But I know you're a coward. You won't cry out."

Karval could not answer. Caught in an iron vise, he followed the Breton. The two men, walking arm in arm, looked like two friends. Kernan headed for the Recouvrance gate. Several times they encountered belated passers-by, but Karval did not dare open his mouth. He felt the point of the sword tearing his clothes.

The streets became more and more deserted. Heavy black clouds made the night very dark. Sometimes Kernan squeezed his companion's arm so hard that muffled cries escaped from his mouth,

"You're hurting me," he said.

"It's nothing," replied the Breton.

Finally they reached the rear entrance to the city, where there was a brightly-lit gate. Karval saw the soldiers on guard coming and going. All he had to do was cry out to make himself heard, but he made no sound.

Ten paces away, the sentinel was walking back and forth. Karval brushed against the soldier as he went by. He only had to make a sign, but he did not do it. Kernan's blade was stabbing into his chest, and a few drops of blood were oozing through his clothing,

Soon the double fortified enclosure was behind them. The two men walked back up the main road for a quarter of a league in total silence, with Karval still firmly attached to Kernan. Then the Breton quickly turned onto a road on his left, and soon arrived at one of the uncultivated fields, surrounded by stones, that form the summit of the high rocks on the coast.

The sea could be heard breaking against the rocks a hundred feet below.

There Kernan stopped.

"Now," he said in a deep voice that indicated his unshakeable resolution and was marked by all his Breton doggedness, "now you are going to die."

"Me?" cried the scoundrel.

Perhaps he wanted to call out then, but his voice stuck in this throat.

"You can shout," said the Breton, "you can beg for mercy, but no one will hear you, not even me. Nothing can save you. If I were you, on my word as a Breton, I would die bravely, not like a coward."

Karval tried to struggle, but the Breton held him with his hand and forced him to the ground.

"Kernan," said Karval, his voice breaking, "have mercy! I'm rich, I have gold. I'll give you a lot of gold. Mercy! Mercy!"

"Mercy for you, you rogue?" cried Kernan in a terrible voice. "You, who with your own hand murdered our good lady, you who with your own hand arrested my lord and had him sentenced to death, you who are going to send our daughter to the guillotine! You renegade Breton, you robber, you arsonist, who have pillaged, ruined, and burned your country! God would damn me, you wretch, if I didn't kill you with my own hand. Now die!"

Karval was lying on the ground and Kernan was raising his hand to strike him, when he stopped. An idea had suddenly crossed his mind. During the war, this same idea often deferred the death of Republican prisoners. It had its origin in the religious sentiment that aroused the masses in the Vendée.

Kernan got to his feet, saying, "You will die, but you won't die without making your confession."

Karval barely understood those words, but after all, with his death postponed, he still had a faint hope of escaping. He could not make a move. Kernan lifted him to his feet with one hand, talking to himself, paying no attention to the wretched Karval.

"Yes, he must confess. I have no right to kill him without his confession. But a priest! Where can I find a priest? I'll even go to Brest to get one if I have to. A priest who has taken the oath. That would be good enough for this villain."

All the while, the Breton was walking, with Karval, like an inert mass, hanging onto his arm and drops of blood marking their passage over the stones in the road.

The walls of Brest soon came into view, however, and Karval, who still cherished the thought of self-preservation, realized what a unique chance lay before him. Once inside the city, he had decided, he would

call for help, even if he were to fall dead. He opened his eyes and saw the ramparts gradually taking shape in the darkness. A few more steps and he would be able to make his last attempt at survival.

At that very moment, at the end of a sunken lane that intersected the main highway, he saw a man passing by. Gathering up his last remaining energy, he broke free of the Breton's grip and ran towards him, shouting, "Save me! Save me!"

But in two jumps, Kernan caught up with him. Looking at the man whom chance had brought before him, he uttered a fierce cry of joy.

"Yvenat!" he cried, "Yvenat the priest! Who would dare to say that God's justice has not played a part in all this, Karval? Listen, it's a priest!"

Karval drew back.

"Yvenat," said Kernan, "I know you. I'm the one who saved you on Tristan Island. You're a priest. This man is condemned to death. Hear his confession."

"But…" said the priest.

"No objections! No hope of mercy. Just do as I say."

Yvenat tried to resist, but Kernan raised his fearsome hand.

"Don't compel me to lay a hand on you. Hear this man's confession. If he can't speak, I'll jog his memory. He's a murderer and a thief. He has only a few minutes left to repent before he appears before God."

There now occurred a terrible scene. The wretched Karval, seeing again in an instant the memories and feelings of his youth and the lessons of his childhood, made a disjointed confession, weeping pitifully, but the Breton was unmoved. Karval did not know what he was saying, while Yvenat, gripped by an irresistible terror, was trembling from head to foot. He could barely hear the words that the penitent pronounced without understanding them. Finally, unable to continue, he gave him a cursory absolution and fled without daring to look back.

He had not yet disappeared around the corner of the sunken road when a sinister cry rang out through the air. Soon the terrified priest could make out a man, carrying another man on his shoulders, slowly cross the deserted fields and hurl a body down from the top of the rocks into the dark waters of the bay.

Chapter XVI

THE 9TH OF THERMIDOR

At midnight, back in Le Portzic, Kernan announced that he had just killed Karval.

Marie went back to her room, shivering. As soon as she had left, the Breton took hold of the chevalier's arm.

"The execution is set for tomorrow," he said.

Henry turned pale with terror.

"It's set for tomorrow," Kernan went on, "but I'll snatch our lord from death's door, even from the scaffold itself, or die in the attempt."

"I'll go with you, Kernan," said Henry.

"And Marie, what will become of her?"

"Marie, Marie," murmured the young man.

"You really must stay here, in case I should happen to die. But don't say anything to the poor girl. Tomorrow she'll be an orphan or she'll have her father back."

Henry tried to insist further, but he was struggling against himself. Both reason and his own feelings determined that he should stay with his fiancée.

Neither Kernan not Henry slept during that fateful night. The Breton prayed fervently.

In the morning, Kernan kissed Marie, shook hands with the chevalier, and set out again for Recouvrance. He had no preconceived plan. The circumstances would determine his actions.

At six o'clock he entered the town and headed for the prison. For two hours he waited. He saw the tumbrel coming, painted red. At eight o'clock it came back out with a load of condemned prisoners, including the Count of Chanteleine, surrounded by the national guards. The mournful procession made its way towards the scaffold.

For a moment, the count caught sight of Kernan in the crowd. A questioning look appeared briefly on his face. What could he be asking, unless it was what had become of his daughter?

A sign from Kernan told him that she was safe. The count must have understood, for a smile came over his face and he began to pray with fervor and deep gratitude.

The tumbrel was moving forward through a large crowd. The town's "sans-culottes," the members of the clubs, all the dregs of the population, were threatening the condemned prisoners and hurling gross insults at them. The count especially, as an aristocrat and a priest, was the target of their most hateful cries of rage.

Kernan was walking along beside the tumbrel. At a turning in the street, the instrument of death appeared, not two hundred paces away.

Suddenly the procession came to a halt and the crowd stopped. Something was happening. People were asking questions, shouting and howling. The words "Enough! Enough!" could be heard.

"Send the condemned prisoners back!"

"Down with the tyrants! Down with Robespierre! Long live the Republic!"

One word explained everything. The 9th of Thermidor had dawned in Paris. The telegraph, which the Convention had adopted two years earlier on Chappe's initiative, had instantaneously brought the great news. Robespierre, Couthon, and Saint-Just had just died on the scaffold.

There was an immediate reaction. Everyone was disgusted with bloodshed. For a moment, pity won out over anger and the deadly tumbrel came to a halt.

Kernan rushed forward at once, and with an irresistible strength removed the count amid cries of "bravo." Half an hour later, the count was in his daughter's arms.

During the few astonishing days that followed the 9th of Thermidor, the count and his family managed to leave the country and finally make their way to England. God had granted these unfortunate people an outcome that they could not have expected from human hands.

Here ends this episode, taken from the darkest days of the Terror. What happened next, everyone can guess.

Henry de Trégolan and Marie were married in England, where the whole family remained for several years.

As soon as emigrants were allowed to return to their homeland, the count was one of the first to go back to France. He returned to Chanteleine with his daughter, Henry, and the loyal Kernan.

There they lived happily and peacefully. The count calmly administered his little parish, preferring that humble role to the high offices that were offered to him. And the fishermen along the coast still speak with regret and gratitude of the noble curé of Chanteleine.

NOTES

by Garmt de Vries-Uiterweerd

MAPS

The locations mentioned in the novel are shown on the three maps that accompany the text. Because of the scale, a few places, such as Paris or Granville, fall outside the maps. It would have been impossible to include all of the locations yet keep the maps legible. The exact situation of the (fictional) Chanteleine Castle cannot be deduced unambiguously from the text: Verne's descriptions are inconsistent. The position as shown on the map was chosen as a reasonable compromise.

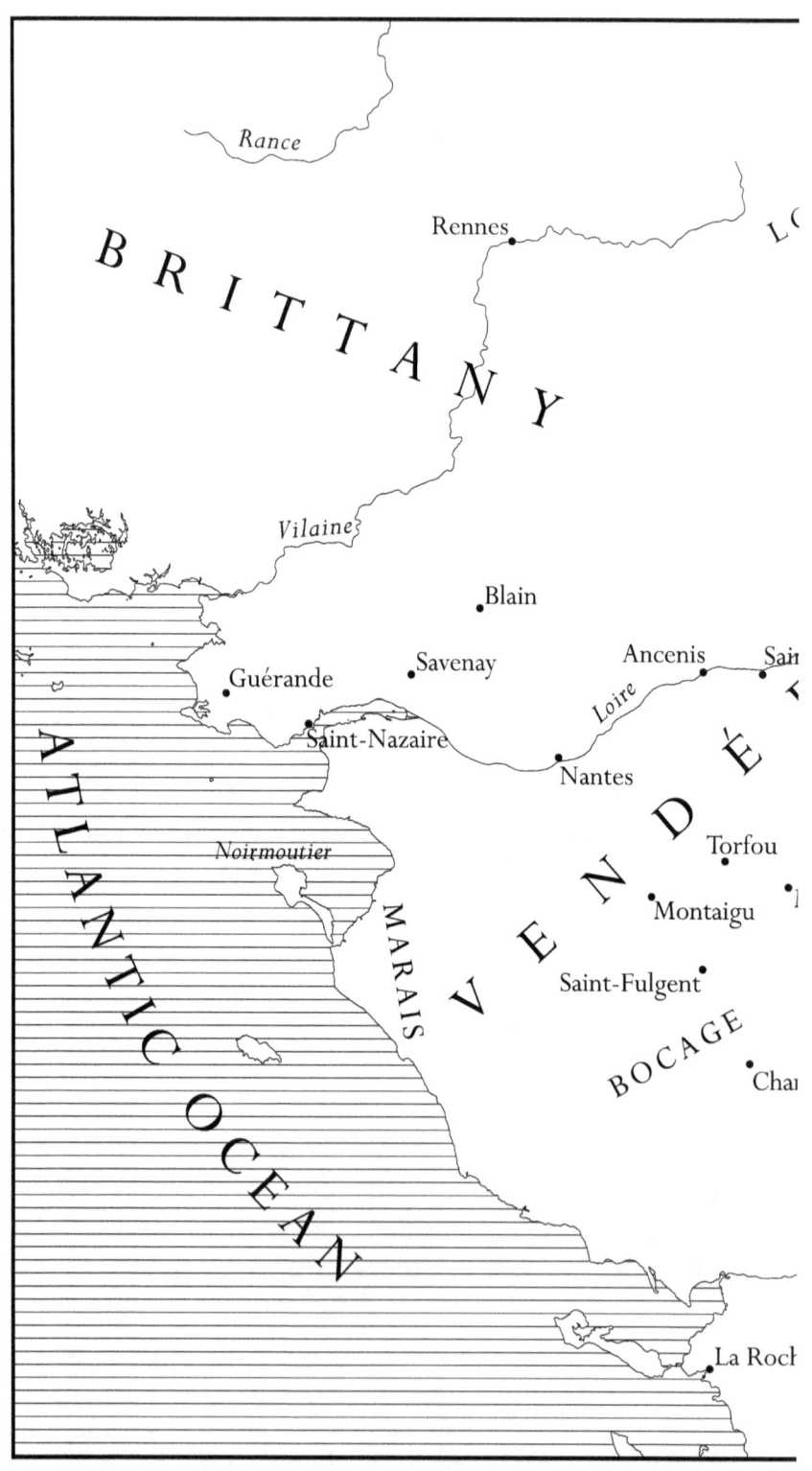

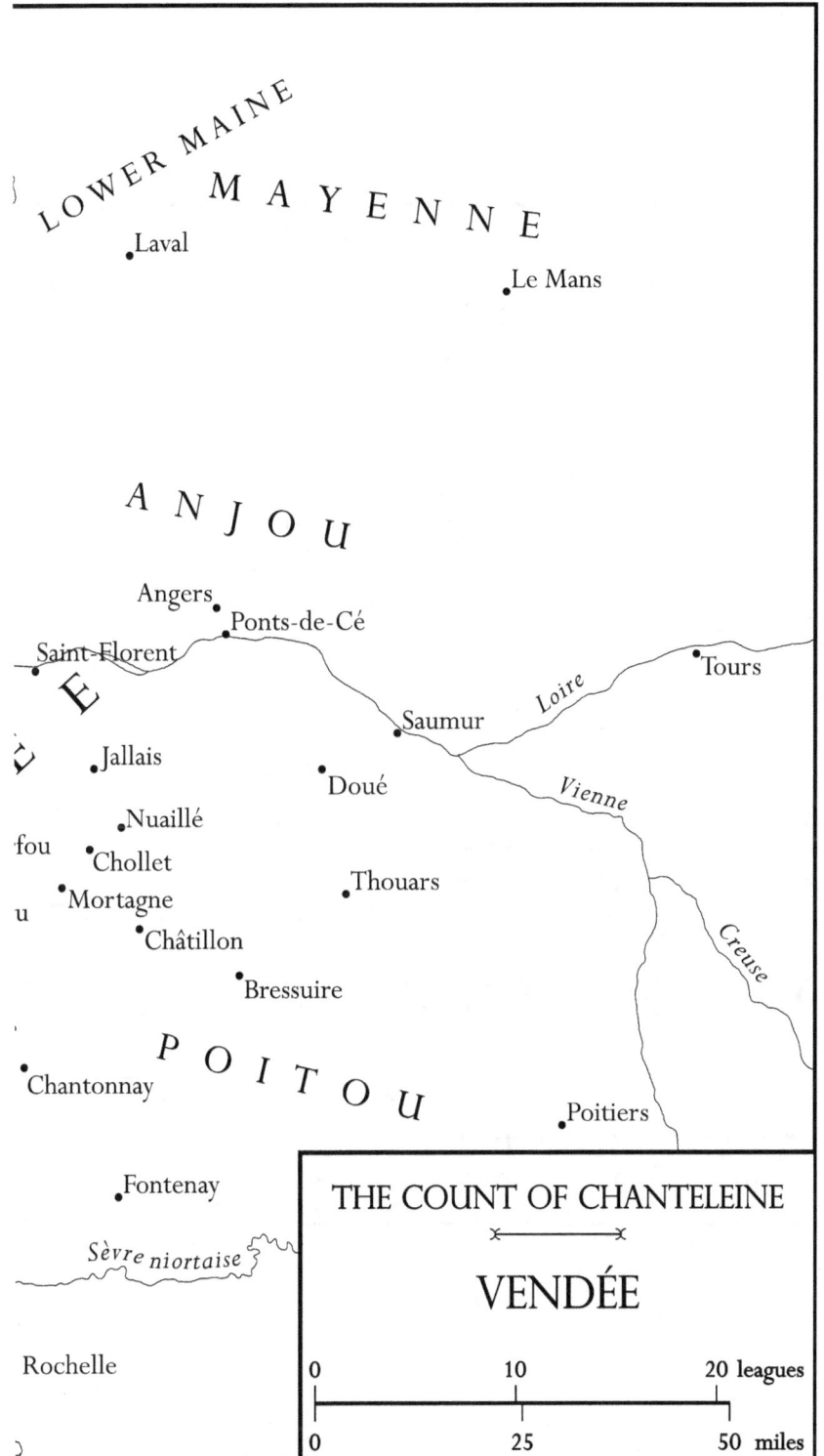

LOWER MAINE

MAYENNE

.Laval

.Le Mans

ANJOU

Angers.
.Ponts-de-Cé
Saint-Florent
.
Tours
Loire
.
Jallais
Saumur
Doué
Vienne
fou
.Nuaillé
.Chollet
.Thouars
u .Mortagne
.Châtillon
Creuse
.Bressuire

POITOU
.Chantonnay
.Poitiers

.Fontenay

Sèvre niortaise

THE COUNT OF CHANTELEINE

VENDÉE

Rochelle

| 0 | 10 | 20 leagues |
| 0 | 25 | 50 miles |

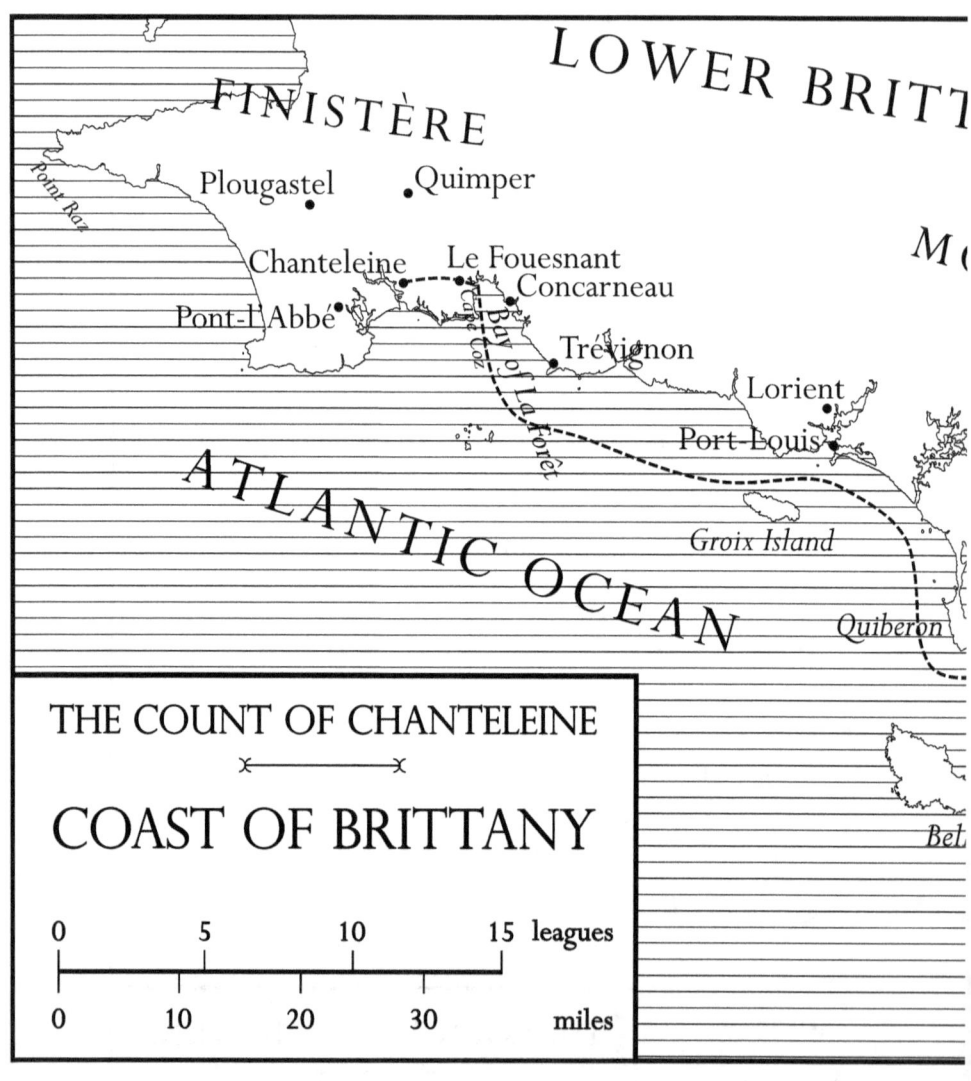

THE COUNT OF CHANTELEINE

COAST OF BRITTANY

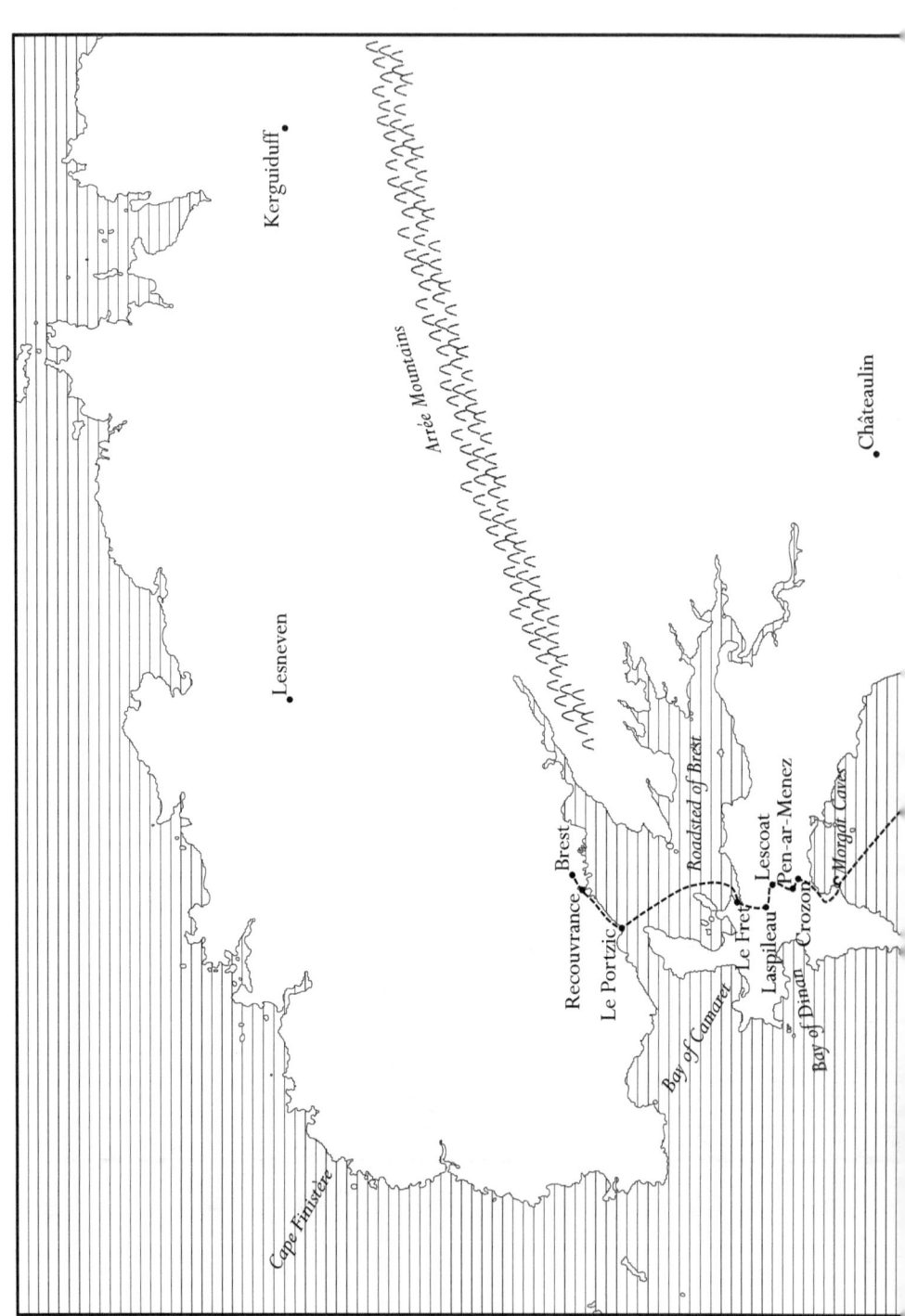

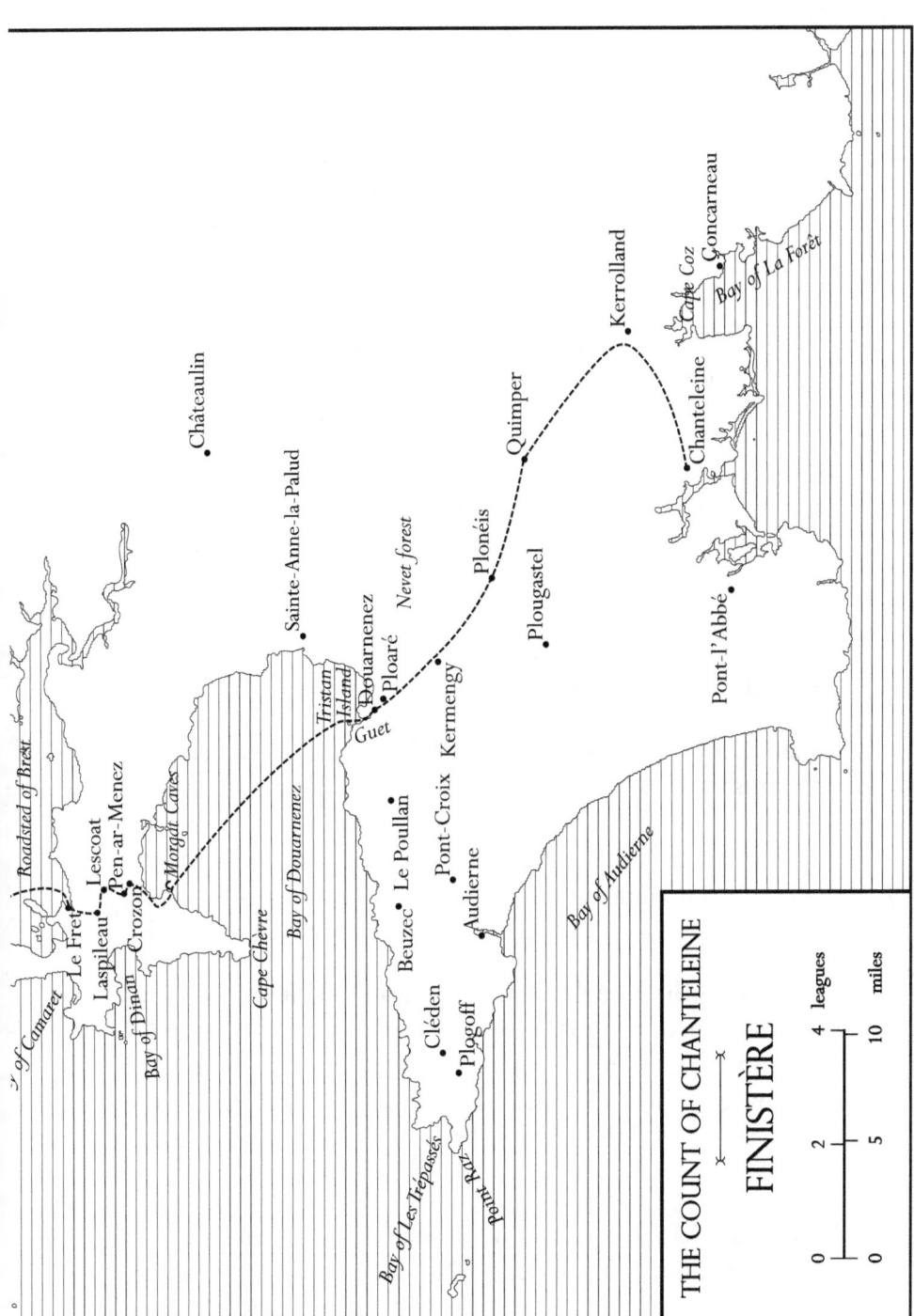

THE COUNT OF CHANTELEINE

FINISTÈRE

Persons

Chapter I

- **Louis XVI** (1754–1793) was king of France from 1774 to 1792. During the course of his reign, power was gradually taken away from him in favor of elected representatives of the people. The Constitution of 1791 made France a constitutional monarchy. After the storming of the Tuileries on August 10, 1792, Louis was arrested. The Republic was proclaimed on September 21. Louis was sentenced to death on charge of high treason, mainly based on his contacts with foreign powers. On January 21, 1793, Louis died under the guillotine.

- **Jacques Cathelineau** (1759–1793), a modest hawker and carter, initiated an armed rebellion on March 10, 1793, after the riots in Saint-Florent-le-Vieil. The rebellion developed into a true campaign, with Cathelineau at the head of several thousand farmers. On June 12, he was chosen supreme commander of the Catholic and Royal Army. He was mortally wounded during the Battle of Nantes on June 29.

- **Jean-Nicolas Stofflet** (1753–1796) began his career as a common soldier, but climbed the ranks to become a general in the Royal Army. He resigned in 1795, because of discord with the other leaders. Later that year he took up arms again, but he was soon taken prisoner and brought before the firing squad.

- **François-Athanase de Charette de La Contrie** (1763–1796) fled to Germany when the Revolution broke out, but returned to France in order to defend the Royal family during the storming of the Tuileries. In 1793, he took command of the rebel farmers of the Marais. Later he left the Catholic and Royal Army and started a guerilla band of his own.

- **Charles Melchior Artus de Bonchamps** (1760–1793), a captain in the French army who had served in America, quit his position after the Revolution. He retired to his castle near Saint-Florent. At the request of the insurgents, he took command of the Vendean army. He was killed at the battle of Chollet.

- **Maurice Joseph Louis Gigost d'Elbée** (1752–1794) was asked by the farmers of Beaupréau, near his estate, to assume control of their rebellion. This group later joined the other rebels in the Vendée. D'Elbée was severely wounded at the battle of Chollet. Three months later, he was arrested and shot by a firing squad, sitting in a chair because of his injuries.

- **Henri de La Rochejaquelein** (1772–1794) joined the insurgents in March 1793 and soon became one of the leaders of the Vendean army, only 20 years old. After D'Elbée and Bonchamps were lost at the battle of Chollet, La Rochejaquelein was chosen as supreme commander. Even after the Catholic and Royal Army had disintegrated, he kept fighting the Republicans. On January 28, 1794, he was shot by a Republican soldier he had overpowered.

- **Louis-Marie de Salgues de Lescure** (1766–1793) was taken prisoner when the uprising in the Vendée broke out. After a few days, he was set free by the Vendean army, which he joined immediately. He distinguished himself for his fearlessness. Having sustained a severe head wound, he followed the retreating troops in a cart. He died on the road to Brittany, after much suffering.

- **Gaspard Augustin René Bernard de Marigny** (1754–1794) was a general in the artillery of the Catholic and Royal Army. He was very popular among his fellows, but harsh towards the enemies he defeated. In 1794, he had a serious feud with Charette and Stofflet and dissociated himself from the other leaders. He was court-martialed and sentenced to death.

- **Jean-Baptiste Annibal Aubert Dubayet** (1757–1797) was a soldier and statesman. He fought in the American War of Independence, became president of the National Constituent Assembly in 1791 and battled alongside Kléber in the siege of Mainz in 1793. He later fought with the Army of Mayençais against the rebels of the Vendée.

- **Jean-Baptiste Kléber** (1753–1800), of common descent, had been vainly pursuing a military career, when the Revolution finally offered him the chance to distinguish himself. Leading the Army of Mayençais, he was able to suppress the rebellion in the Vendée.

- **Jean Baptiste Camille de Canclaux** (1740–1817) had obtained the rank of field marshal under the Ancien Régime. As a general, he fought the Vendean insurgents. During the battle of Nantes, he held out against the superior numbers of the rebels, but a later defeat at Tiffauges made him lose his post.

- **Antoine-Joseph Santerre** (1752–1809) played an important role during the storming of the Bastille in 1789, the storming of the Tuileries in 1792, the September massacres later that year, and the execution of Louis XVI in 1793. He served as a general in the Vendée for several months.

- **François-Séverin Marceau** (1769–1796) enrolled in the army as a young man. During the fighting in the Ardennes, he was noted for his loyalty. His magnanimous conduct earned him the rank of general.

- **François-Joseph Westermann** (1751–1794) took part in the storming of the Tuileries in 1792. A general of the Republican army, he was a fearsome and cruel opponent of the rebels in the West. He was nicknamed "the butcher of the Vendée."

- **Dominique-Louis Piron de La Varenne** (1755–1794) was one of the leaders of the Catholic and Royal Army. He distinguished himself at the battle of Vihiers. Attempting to cross the Loire, he was killed when his boat was fired upon.

- **François de Lyrot de La Patouillère** (1723–1793), of petty nobility, was elected mayor of Saint-Sébastien in 1790. In the early months of 1793, at the age of 69, he joined the insurgents in the Vendée. He fell in the battle of Savenay, covering the retreat of the fugitives.

- **Jacques Nicolas Fleuriot de La Fleuriais** (1738–1824) was the right hand man of Bonchamps and later served under Stofflet. After the crossing of the Loire at Ancenis, he led the remaining troups to Blain and Savenay. Having escaped the massacre of Savenay, he fought for a while under Charette.

- **Armand-Michel Bacharetie de Beaupuy** (1755–1796) was from an aristocratic family, but sided with the Republicans after the Revolution, serving with the Army of Mayençais in the battle of Savenay. He later declared he found fighting his fellow countrymen repulsive.

Chapter II

- **Jean-Baptiste Carrier** (1756–1794) had been sent to Nantes by the National Convention in order to quash the insurrection. He conducted an extremely cruel reign of terror; prisoners were decapitated or shot by the hundreds. He also drowned thousands of rebels in the Loire, which was nicknamed "the Republican river".

- **Jean Cottereau** (1757–1794) and his brothers took part in the counterrevolutionary insurrection in Brittany. In the autumn of 1793, he fought in the Vendean army; after the defeat at Le Mans he retreated to Lower Maine, where he continued his struggle and led a new rebellion in 1794.

Chapter III

- **Madame de Lescure**, née Victoire de Donnissan (1772–1857) was the daughter of Guy Joseph de Donnissan de Citran and the wife of Louis-Marie de Salgues de Lescure. She followed her husband during the revolt in the Vendée and nursed him during the flight to Brittany, after he had been severely injured. After the Bourbon Restoration, she published her memoirs under the name Victoire de Donnissan de La Rochejaquelein.

- **Madame de Donnissan**, née Marie Françoise de Durfort Civrac (1747–1837) was the wife of Guy Joseph de Donnissan de Citran. In 1791, the family fled revolutionary Paris. Donnissan served as general in the Vendean army and was later named president of the Conseil Vendéen. His wife and daughter accompanied him, but the family was separated during the battle of Savenay. Despite terrible ordeals, both women survived the war.

Chapter IV

- **Louis XIII** (1601–1643) was king of France and Navarre, and the father of Louis XIV, the Sun King.

- **Louis XII** (1462–1515) was the great-grandson of Charles V. In 1498, he succeeded his cousin Charles VIII, who had died without issue, as king of France.

- **Anne de Bretagne** (1477–1514) became duchess of the de facto independent duchy of Brittany following her father's death in 1488. Three years later, after a brief war, she was forced to marry Charles VIII of France. After Charles's death, she had to marry his successor Louis XII, according to an article in the marriage contract. This union marked the beginning of the annexation of Brittany by the French kings, a process that was finished in 1532 with the Edict of Union.

- **Philippe Auguste**, as Philippe II (1165–1223) is generally known, took part in the third crusade in 1190–91.

- **Alain Nédellec** (1757/1758–1793), a peasant from Le Fouesnant, was elected justice of the peace in 1790. His loyalty to the king and discord with the patriots of Quimper led to an armed revolt of the farmers in Le Fouesnant, which was brutally suppressed by the National Guard of Quimper. Nédellec was taken prisoner and sentenced to death. In March 1793 he was guillotined, the first in Quimper to meet this fate.

Chapter V

- **Toussaint-François-Joseph Conen de Saint-Luc** (1724–1790) was bishop of Cornouaille from 1773. He was a fierce opponent of the Civil Constitution of the Clergy. He died on September 30, 1790, shortly after the Constitution had been voted upon. His successor was the first bishop to be appointed in accordance with the new rules.

- **François Louis de Kergariou du Cosquer** (1725–1794) was an administrator of the department Finistère after the 1790 elections. He cautioned the excessively radical groups in Paris, and after the fall of the Girondins he sent an armed force to Paris in order to enforce a more moderate policy. On May 22, 1794, he was executed along with 25 other administrators who were responsible for this action.

- **Jean-Paul Marat** (1743–1793) was a surgeon, scientist, journalist, and one of the most radical members of the National Convention. In his publications he called for an unconciliatory position towards the enemies of the Republic. His flaming pleas are considered to have contributed to the September massacres of 1792. On July 13, 1793, Marat was killed by Charlotte Corday while taking a bath.

- **Jacques Tanguy Marie Guermeur** (1750–1798) was a member of the National Convention for the department of Finistère. He was sent to Brittany to restore order in the region. Among other measures, he replaced the local authorities with candidates more to the liking of the National Convention.

- **Marc-Antoine Jullien** (1775–1848) was a representative on a mission for the Committee of Public Safety whose drastic actions repressed the federalists and Royalists.

- **Philippe-Antoine Merlin de Douai** (1754–1838) drafted many laws as a member of the National Constituent Assembly and of the National Convention. After Robespierre's downfall, to which he had contributed, Merlin was president of the Convention and a member of the Committee of Public Safety. He remained an influential politician under Napoléon.

Chapter VI

- **Mutius Scévola** is the French orthography of Mucius Scaevola, a legendary Roman soldier. After Tarquinius Superbus, the last king of Rome, had been expelled in 509 BC, his Etruscan allies, under the command of Porsenna, besieged the city. Gaius Mucius Scaevola penetrated the Etruscan camp with the aim of killing Porsenna. He was apprehended and threatened with torture, but he put his hand in the fire of his own free will, proving that physical harm did not frighten him.

- **Guislain-François-Joseph Le Bon** (1765–1795) was a representative on a mission for the Committee of Public Safety in the departments of Somme and Pas-de-Calais, from which he carried out the Terror. After the 9th of Thermidor, he was guillotined himself.

- **Georges Auguste Couthon** (1755–1794) was a representative in the National Convention. Initially, he kept away from the strife between Gironde and Montagne, but in due course he joined the latter faction, on account of his friendship with Robespierre. As a member of the Committee of Public Safety he reformed justice, abolishing interrogation, defense and the hearing of witnesses. After the 9th of Thermidor, he was executed together with Robespierre and Saint-Just.

Chapter IX

- **Saint Anne** was the mother of the Virgin Mary. In the Catholic tradition, she is the patron saint of seamstresses and lacemakers. She is also the patron saint of Brittany.

- **Sophie Céleste Eléonore de Sapinaud de la Rairie** (1770–1854), nicknamed "La Belle Vendéenne," was the daughter of Charles Daniel de Sapinaud, one of the leaders of the Catholic and Royal Army. Together with her two sisters and her cousin Marie de Lézardière, she accompanied her father during his campaigns. She was separated from her father in the flight from Le Mans; he was killed shortly afterwards. The memoirs of Sophie de Sapinaud were published by one of her descendants in 1925.

- **Marie Charlotte Pauline de Lézardière** (1754–1835) was born into an old and noble family. She wrote the thorough study *La Théorie des Lois politiques de la Monarchie française*, which was printed in 1791, but only published in 1801 due to the troubles of the Revolution. Her family suffered much: her mother died of grief at the execution of Louis XVI and two of her brothers, who fought in the Vendean army under La Rochejaquelein, willingly surrendered in exchange for the life of their father, who had been arrested for their actions. Mademoiselle de Lézardière withdrew from public life to care for her father.

Chapter XI

- **Knud II** (994/995–1035), or Canute in English, was king of Denmark and, after the invasion of 1016, king of England. He is mostly famous for the legend according to which he placed his throne on the beach and vainly ordered the waves to retreat. He wanted to demonstrate that not even he could command the sea, as some flattering courtiers would have it. Jules Verne probably confuses king Canute with king **Gradlon**, the founder of the legendary city of Ys. This city lay below sea level and was protected by a mighty dike. One day, Gradlon's licentious, heathen daughter Dahut stole the keys to the sluice that closed the dike and handed them over to her lover, who was in fact the devil himself. The sluice was opened and the city was engulfed by the sea.

Chapter XII

- **Georges Jacques Danton** (1759–1794) was made minister of justice after the abolition of the monarchy. Together with Marat and Robespierre he formed a sort of triumvirate, but his moderate attitude brought him into open conflict with Robespierre. Danton was arrested on the order of the Committee of Public Safety and after a brief show trial, he was guillotined on April 5, 1794.

- **Napoléon Bonaparte** (1769–1821) was a lieutenant in the army when the Revolution broke out. He reached the rank of general, became a consul after the 1799 coup d'etat, and crowned himself Emperor in 1804. After many military successes, the tide turned with the disastrous invasion of Russia in 1812. Napoléon was finally defeated in the battle of Waterloo in 1815. He spent his last years in exile on Saint Helena.

- **Joseph-Marie de Maistre** (1753–1821) was a lawyer, writer, and philosopher. He was a great proponent of monarchy, which he regarded as the only stable form of government, in that it was based on divine justice. To cast doubt on the legitimacy of the power of the king could, according to De Maistre, only lead to chaos and bloodshed, as had been proven by the French Revolution.

- **François-René de Chateaubriand** (1768–1848) was a politician and author, one of the exponents of French Romanticism. He was an ardent monarchist. During the Bourbon Restoration, he served several times as minister and ambassador.

- **Bertrand Barère de Vieuzac** (1755–1841) was a representative in the National Constituent Assembly and later in the National Convention. Initially a moderate member of the Plaine, he sympathised more and more with Robespierre's faction. In the Committee of Public Safety he was responsible for diplomacy, education, and arts.

- **Jacques Nicolas Billaud-Varenne** (1756–1819) was a member of the National Convention for the Montagne. In this position, and later as a member of the Committee of Public Safety, he was a fierce proponent of the Terror. Later, he quarreled with Robespierre and became largely responsible for his downfall.

- **Lazare Nicolas Marguerite Carnot** (1753–1823) was one of the more moderate members of the Committee of Public Safety. He reorganized the army and was responsible for several important military successes in campaigns that he sometimes led in person.

- **Jean-Marie Collot d'Herbois** (1749–1796) was a member of the National Convention for the Montagne and an ardent advocate of the Terror. As a member of the Committee of Public Safety, he was responsible for the communication with its representatives on missions. He was sent to Lyon to punish the federalist insurrection in that city, a task which he carried out with extraordinary cruelty.

- **Pierre-Louis Prieur** (1756–1827), sometimes called Prieur de la Marne, was a member of the Committee of Public Safety, responsible for the navy. As a representative, he spent most of his time on a mission in the provinces, including the Vendée and in Brittany.

- **Jean-Baptiste Robert Lindet** (1746–1825) was a Montagnard, but maintained a moderate attitude within the Committee of Public Safety. Responsible for finances and supplies, he took measures against the famine that threatened Paris at the end of 1793.

- **Maximilien Marie Isidore de Robespierre** (1758–1794), sometimes called Robespierre the elder to distinguish him from his younger brother Augustin Bon Joseph de Robespierre, was one of the leading figures of the Revolution. As a member of the National Constituent Assembly, he strove for equality of rights and general suffrage. Robespierre became one the most important members of the Montagne. After struggles with the Girondins and later with Danton, Robespierre, who had joined the Committee of Public Safety, became more and more powerful and tyrannical. The excesses of the Terror, during which nobody could be certain of his life, led to his downfall. Robespierre was arrested on July 27, 1794 and executed without trial.

- **Louis Antoine Léon de Saint-Just** (1767–1794) was the youngest representative in the National Convention and one of those closest to Robespierre. He contributed to Danton's downfall and to the reform of military justice. After the 9th of Thermidor, he was executed together with Robespierre and Couthon.

- **André Jeanbon Saint-André** (1749–1813) was initially affiliated with the Gironde, but soon switched sides to join the Montagne. He was mostly absent from Paris and tried to stay clear of the strife and struggle between the factions.

- **Claude-Antoine Prieur-Duvernois** (1763–1832), better known as Prieur de la Côte-d'Or, was an officer of the Engineers and one of the proponents of the metric system. Together with Carnot, he mainly took care of the technical aspects of warfare.

- **Marie-Jean Héraut de Séchelles** (1759–1794) was a representative in the Legislative Assembly and in the National Convention, and a member of several committees. His close ties with Danton led to his execution in April 1794, along with other Dantonists.

- **Louis Marie Turreau** (1756–1816) was a general in the Republican army. He received orders to punish the rebels in the Vendée. To that end, he organized the infernal columns, which roamed the country, bringing death and destruction upon the inhabitants.

- **Louis Grignon** (1748–1825) was a Brigade General and leader of the second division of the infernal columns, one of the most murderous and ruthless of the six divisions.

- **Antoine-Philippe de la Trémoille, prince of Talmont** (1765–1794) was a member of an illustrious noble family. After two botched attempts at counter-revolutionary conspiracies, he travelled to the western provinces. There he tried to raise forces and soon joined the Catholic and Royal Army. After the army was destroyed, he attempted to get in touch with Jean Chouan, but he was arrested and executed.

- **Nicolas Haxo** (1749–1794) served in the National Guard and was a volunteer at the front, where he soon became a general. The victories at Chollet and Noirmoutier were mainly due to him. He was killed in a fight with Charette's troops.

Chapter XVI

- **Claude Chappe** (1763–1805) was a clergyman and scientist. As a young man, he published several scientific articles. Together with his four brothers he developed the optical telegraph. Chappe committed suicide in 1805, suffering from depression.

HISTORICAL REFERENCES, ORGANIZATIONS, AND EVENTS

Chapter I

- The **National Convention** (*Convention nationale*) succeeded the Legislative Assembly as the legislative power of France on September 21, 1792. Its first act was the proclamation of the Republic. Its 749 members could be divided into three groups. The **Montagne** favored a radical approach with firm action against the counterrevolution. The **Girondins** were more moderate and attached more value to personal liberties. The third and largest group, the **Plaine** (also known as Marais), occupied the center, sometimes voting along with the Gironde, sometimes with the Montagne. A struggle for power soon arose between Gironde and Montagne. The latter prevailed, and under their influence, the Convention showed an increasing harshness towards the opponents of the Revolution.

- **Constitutional priests** were those priests who had sworn allegiance to the Civil Constitution of the Clergy, which had been adopted on July 12, 1790. This constitution made the Roman Catholic Church in France subordinate to the government; bishops and priests were henceforth elected democratically. Priests who refused to take the oath were prosecuted vigorously.

- **Conscription** was introduced because of the military threat from the coalition of European powers against the Revolution. In the past, there had only been a professional army, supplemented with volunteers.

- The **national guard** was a militia of civilians which was formed in each city. After the proclamation of the Republic in 1792, the national guard sided with the revolutionaries. During the war with the allied forces, the national guard was used more and more as reserve troops for the army.

- The **Catholic and Royal Army** (*Armée catholique et royale*) is the name that came into use during the year 1793 for the army of insurrectionists in the Vendée. The army consisted of various groups of rebels, in an ever-changing composition.

- The terms **Whites** and **Blues** were used for Royalists and Republicans, respectively.

- The **Mayençais** (or Mainz) army was one of the Republican armies. It consisted of the garrison that had been taken prisoner at the Siege of Mainz and had been released by the allied forces on the condition that it would not do battle anymore. The army was sent to the Vendée to help suppress the insurrection.

- The **Committee of Public Safety** (*Comité de salut public*) was created by the National Convention on April 6, 1793, allowing the country to be governed energetically in times of war and rebellion. The executive power was completely in the hands of the Committee, which, under Robespierre, was responsible for the Terror.

- The bloody reprisals in the Vendée, and the assignment to the Mayençais to **create a desert**, are still a topic of debate among historians. Some view the massacres and destructions as genocide, others find that claim too strong. Even the number of victims is not accurately known, but most estimates lie around 150,000.

- The **Republican calendar** was adopted in 1792 and remained in use, with a few adaptations, until 1806. The year was divided into twelve months, with names inspired by weather and agriculture. Each month was thirty days long, divided into three decades of ten days each. The year ended with five (or six, in leap years) separate days, the *sansculottides*.

Chapter II

- The **livre** (pound) was a unit of currency under the Ancien Régime. Originally, one *livre* had been worth exactly a pound of silver, but over the course of history, its value decreased significantly. By the late 18th century, there was no relation at all anymore between weight and value.

- The **festivals of Brittany** are a typical regional custom. The devout population makes a pilgrimage to a church, chapel or other place dedicated to their patron saint, to do penance. The ceremony is followed by festive activities, of which wrestling matches are traditionally an important part.

- The term **league** is used for several different measures of distance. The league used here is probably the *lieue de Paris* of the Ancien Régime, which is equivalent to 2.423 miles.

- In 1789, active citizens obtained the right of assembly. Soon, **Republican clubs** were formed, which developed into influential political associations, where political, legal, and sociological issues were discussed.

- The sale of confiscated land did not yield sufficient means for the Legislative Assembly to reduce the national debt. Hence, in 1790, a large quantity of bonds was issued, which were soon declared legal tender. The confidence in these *assignats* was low, and within a few years they were practically **worthless paper**.

- The **louis** was a currency under the Ancien Régime, equivalent to 24 *livres*.

Chapter III

- In 1795, the peninsula of **Quiberon** was the scene of a bloody battle. British troops and French emigrants landed on Quiberon with the aim to raise a rebellion throughout the West, and to restore monarchy. After almost a month of fighting, the Republicans stormed the peninsula on July 20. The British ships could do nothing but withdraw. The Royalists capitulated, but they were shot by firing squads, hundreds at a time, in spite of promises made by the Republicans.

Chapter IV

- A **machicolation** is a square hole in a battlement, through which stones, burning tar, and the like, could be thrown on assailants below.

- The **Municipalities** were city councils comprised of civilians, which the revolutionaries had created in the larger cities.

- The **municipal prosecutor** (*procureur-général syndic*) represented the executive power in the newly created departments. In practice, this official had only little power. The office was abolished in 1793.

- The French Revolution was rich in iconography. Paintings, drawings, statues and bas-reliefs contained many symbols representing the core values of the Revolution, often taken from antiquity or freemasonry. In early history, the **eye** stood for the All-seeing God (in that context it was often enclosed in a triangle), but also for reason, vigilance and justice. During the Revolution, it symbolised justice by the sovereign state, which was always wakeful. **Bundles of pikes and branches** referred to the unity and indivisibility of the Republic and to the strength that resulted from this unity. In combination with an axe, these fasces stood for the state's authority. Obviously, the connotation of fascism as it developed in the 20th century did not yet exist. The **Phrygian bonnet** was a kind of cap of Far Eastern origin, which historically symbolized freedom. In 1791 the bonnet came into vogue in France as a sign of liberty and citizenship.

Chapter V

- On **August 10, 1792,** the palace of the Tuileries was stormed. The night before, the Parisian city council was replaced with a new council, whose members were representatives of the sections of Paris. The sections decided, almost unanimously, to depose the king. The next morning, a large army marched on the palace, where a fierce battle with the Swiss Guards took place. The king, who had fled to the nearby building of the Legislative Assembly, was taken prisoner.

- **Federalism** was the idea, mainly supported by the Girondins, that the 83 French departments, which had replaced the provinces of the Ancien Régime in 1790, should form a federation of equal states. In order to strengthen the ties between the departments and the state, and to prevent the possible secession of individual departments, the Feast of the Federation was held in Paris on July 14, 1790. One hundred thousand representatives from all departments assembled on the Champ de Mars to swear allegiance to the nation and to the law. Later, the Montagne turned against the federalists, who advocated a relatively large autonomy for the departments. After the downfall of Girondins in 1793, federalism was prohibited.

- The **Legislative Assembly** (*Assemblée législative*) was the parliament that was created by the 1791 constitution. It was in force from October 1, 1791, to September 21, 1792. The Assembly had 745 members, all newly elected, since members of its predecessor, the National Constituent Assembly, could not be reelected. The Legislative Assembly decided on laws, taxes, treaties, and declarations of war. The king only had a suspensive veto.

- On July 11, 1792, the Legislative Assembly declared **"the fatherland is in danger"** because of the imminent invasion by the allied powers, who wished to crush the Revolution and to restore the king to his full powers.

- The **Breton Club** had a major influence on the early beginnings of the Revolution. It was founded by a group of representatives from Brittany, who discussed beforehand the issues that were going to be debated in the Estates General. Since Brittany had always continued to call meetings of its Estates, the members of the Breton Club were very experienced and put forward many detailed proposals.

- The **Jacobin Club** was created in October, 1789, when the Breton Club was reformed. The club soon developed from a discussion group for deputies into a stage for radical revolutionaries, with considerable political influence. In the early days, both Girondins and Montagnards were members of the club, but after the proclamation of the Republic, the club was ruled more and more by Robespierre. The Jacobins never recovered from Robespierre's downfall and were closed in November, 1794.

- In 1790, the National Constituent Assembly divided Paris into 48 **sections**. These replaced the districts that had been created for the 1789 elections.

- The **Society of the Friends of the Constitution** (*Amis de la Constitution*) in Paris was the successor of the Breton Club. It was located in the convent of the Jacobins, from which it would soon take its new name, Jacobin Club. Throughout the country, local sections were formed, which copied the organisation and the name of the Friends of the Constitution in Paris.

- The **Cordeliers** were a Franciscan order. Their convents were closed and confiscated by the state in 1790.

- The **Declaration of the Rights of Man** was written in 1789. The text lists a number of fundamental and universal natural rights, that each human being enjoys: liberty, property, safety and resistance against oppression. The Declaration had a large influence on the successive French constitutions.

- The newspaper *L'Ami du Peuple*—a "political, free and impartial journal," according to its subtitle—was a publication by Jean-Paul Marat, who used it to spread his vehement commentaries. *L'Ami du Peuple* appeared from September, 1789 to September, 1792.

- The **Paris Commune** was called *Commune* and not, as in other cities, *Municipalité*, because there had already been a *Municipalité* under the Ancien Régime.

- A **proconsul** was a representative of the central authority, who held the executive power in a certain area.

- The **Fort du Taureau** is a fortress on a small island in the Bay of Morlaix. It was built in 1542 and has frequently been reconstructed and enlarged. In the 18th century the fortress also served as a prison.

- The struggle for power between Montagne and Gironde reached a climax on June 2, 1793. There were riots in the city and the Commune forced the National Convention, under the threat of cannon, to expel 29 Girondins and two ministers from the assembly. The representatives who later protested against this forcefully obtained decision were arrested. The **execution of 21 Girondins** followed in October, after a brief and unfair trial.

- The **Terror** was a period during which opponents of the Revolution were violently repressed. Tens of thousands of suspects were guillotined or summarily executed. A first period of Terror occurred from the storming of the Tuileries on August 10, 1792 until the proclamation of the Republic on September 20. In this period, the executive power was in the hands of the insurrectional Paris Commune. After the downfall of the Girondins in June, 1793, a second period of Terror commenced. The Law on Suspects made it simple to arrest opponents. In the summer of 1794, even the hearing of witnesses was abolished. The Terror ended with the execution of Robespierre.

- The term **sans-culotte** refers to revolutionaries of modest descent, like craftsmen or shopkeepers, who often had radical opinions. The name comes from the fact that these people did not wear breeches (*culottes*).

- The **Law on Suspects**, which was adopted on September 17, 1793, made it easier to arrest and try enemies of the Revolution. It was an important instrument of the Terror. Emigrants and refractory priests had already been automatically suspect; the decree of 1793 significantly broadened the number of grounds for suspicion.

- *Ça ira* was a revolutionary song, whose lyrics were written in 1790 to an existing tune. The chorus is: "Ah ! ça ira, ça ira, ça ira ! Les aristocrates à la lanterne ! Ah ! ça ira, ça ira, ça ira ! Les aristocrates, on les pendra !"

- The date **6th of Nivôse, Year II of the Republic** corresponds to December 26, 1793.

Chapter VI

- The triangle was a symbol taken from the freemasons, which represented equality. It was often depicted alongside a Marianne, the allegorical figure who personified the Republic. In popular parlance, the term **"egalitarian triangle"** was sometimes also used as a reference to the guillotine because of the triangular shape of the blade.

- The **Chouans** were rebels in the west of France, who fought the Republicans more or less at the same time as the insurrection in the Vendée. After a first series of skirmishes, the *chouannerie* was put down in March, 1793. In autumn, the Chouans temporarily joined the Catholic and Royal Army. Later they often withdrew to their own regions, where they fought a guerilla war.

- The **guillotine** is a decapitation machine with a heavy blade that falls down between two upright wooden poles and swiftly cuts through the victim's neck. The apparatus was developed by the doctors Antoine Louis and Joseph-Ignace Guillotin as a more reliable and humane alternative to the traditional methods of execution, such as hanging or decapitation by the sword.

Chapter IX

- The chapel of **Sainte-Anne-la-Palud** in the village of the same name dates from the Middle Ages, although it has frequently been restructured. Saint Anne was venerated in this area as early as the 6ᵗʰ century. The chapel was an important place of pilgrimage, especially in the 18ᵗʰ century.

Chapter XII

- The **Legitimist Party** was a Royalist movement, which took the simple Salic law (succession exclusively in the male line) as the leading principle in the choice of the king. It therefore favored the House of Bourbon over the House of Orleans.

- The **infernal columns** were a military operation aimed at punishing the insurgents and definitively repressing any form of resistance, after the Catholic and Royal Army had been scattered. The columns traversed the country according to itineraries that had been fixed in advance, systematically massacring the population, burning down villages and destroying fields and forests. In a few months' time, it is estimated that the infernal columns left over 100,000 victims in its wake.

- Jean-Baptiste Carrier allegedly used specially constructed **boats equipped with valves** for the mass drownings in Nantes, but it is not clear whether this really did happen.

Chapter XIII

- The **écu** was a French coin under the Ancien Régime, equivalent to six *livres*.

Chapter XVI

- The date **9ᵗʰ of Thermidor** (July 27) has become synonymous with the downfall of Robespierre and the political changes that came with it. Because of conflicts within the Committee of Public Safety, Robespierre had not attended its meetings for almost a month. On July 26, 1794, he proposed that the National Convention to change the composition of the Committee. His opponents, however, managed to win the majority in the Convention for their cause and during a tumultuous meeting on July 27, Robespierre was arrested. His execution on the following day signalled the end of the Terror and the beginning of a transition to a more stable form of government under the Directoire.

- The (optical) **telegraph** was a telecommunication system based on lines of watchtowers, placed at intervals of up to 15 miles and equipped with wooden arms on a mast. These arms could be positioned in various configurations in order to relay signals. In this manner, information could travel much faster than with a courier on a horse. Actually, the line between Paris and Brest was only inaugurated in 1798.

Afterword

JULES VERNE'S FORGOTTEN TRIP ACROSS BRITTANY

by Volker Dehs

It is commonplace to say that Jules Verne didn't make the travels described in his sixty "Voyages Extraordinaires" ("Extraordinary Journeys"), so if literary fiction must exhaustingly and directly represent personal experience, his own artistic claim is reduced. On the other hand, we know that Verne used reminiscences of all of his trips in writing some of his novels and short stories. One of his diaries, actually preserved in the Amiens Municipal Library in France and still unpublished, is almost entirely devoted to a trip across Scandinavia in summer 1861.[1] The notes on blue paper are difficult to decipher because hastily written with pencil; they were largely used for writing two novels, the fragment of *Joyeuses Misères de trois voyageurs en Scandinavie* (*Merry Miseries of Three Travellers in Scandinavia*, written in 1861, published only in 2003) and *Un Billet de loterie* (*A Lottery Ticket*, 1886). Between these notes (almost 80 pages, including 17 sketches, some of them very fine) and those on a short travel to Cannes in 1865 or 1866 (in fact, one date rectifies the other), we find eleven pages on a trip that had not been mentioned before by French or English Verne biographers.

---

1. JV MS 12. This is a leather-bound notebook with 74 sheets (written recto/verso, around 20 sheets are blank) and a metal closure. The book bears two original labels, one in English: "Henry Penny's Patent Improved Metallic Books", the second in French: "Laroche aîné / Rue de Provence N° 40". The whole manuscript is intended to be placed online in 2011.

Under the title "Paris to Brest," Verne took notes on a trip across Brittany, with stations that obviously recall some of the important locations of the story *The Count of Chanteleine*: Brest, Douarnenez, Morgat caves, Porzic, and Le Havre. Half of the pages are covered with sketches of edifices and landscapes: Brest Cathedral and roadstead, Tristan Island, Douarnenez, the fortress and lighthouse of Porzic, even a little draft of the Confederate vessel *Florida,* where Verne had dined with its captain during his visit to Brest and Le Havre. Some years later, in 1869, Verne uses a ship with this name in a tragic scene of *Vingt Mille Lieues sous les mers* (*Twenty Thousand Leagues under the Sea*, 1869; first part, chapter 19).

In his notes, Verne is interested in landscape details, history and legends. He refers to the legend of the submerged city of Ys, even quoting it with erroneous attribution in *The Count of Chanteleine*. There is no doubt that Verne used these notes in writing his story—but when? The only date given is in the beginning of the notes: "Saturday 22, started at Rennes at 6:30 a.m.," but no further detail is provided to specify month and year. A Saturday the 22 occurred in February, March and November, 1862, in August 1863, and October 1864. Fortunately, a cursory note in a letter to his publisher Pierre-Jules Hetzel can solve this problem: "Je suis de retour d'une excursion de quinze jours à Brest" ("I have returned from a fifteen day excursion to Brest"), he wrote on September 4, 1863.[2]

Consequently and logically, "Saturday 22" can be attributed to August 1863. Unfortunately, the manuscript of *The Count of Chanteleine* is still missing, like most of the texts written for the magazine *Musée des Familles* between 1851 and 1871. The autograph could probably provide further information on the circumstances of the writing. However, the chronological situation of Verne's Britanny trip shows that *The Count of Chanteleine* is on no account a youthful work, but was written immediately before its publication in 1864, in any case after *Cinq semaines en ballon* (*Five Weeks in a Balloon*, 1863) and simultaneously with *Voyages et aventures du capitaine Hatteras* (*The Journeys and Adventures of Captain Hatteras*, 1866) and the correction of *Paris au XXᵉ siècle* (*Paris in the Twentieth Century*, which remained unpublished until 1994). The presence of a cemetery scene in both *The*

---

2.   Olivier Dumas, Piero Gondolo della Riva, and Volker Dehs, eds. *Correspondance inédite de Jules Verne et de Pierre-Jules Hetzel (1863-1886)*, vol. 1 (1863-1874) (Geneva: Slatkine, 1999), 22.

Count of Chanteleine and *Paris in the Twentieth Century* could be an indication to the proximity of their composition.

The magazine of publication, *Musée des familles*, suggests another reason for its relatively recent composition. In this conservative magazine, Verne had published his first short stories since 1851. After 1855, however, with the publication of *Un hivernage dans les glaces* (*A Winter Amid the Ice*), there is a gap which is difficult to explain. Two other stories of Verne, *Un Radeau sur le Rhin* and *Aventures en Calabre* (*A Raft on the Rhine* and *Adventures in Calabria*), had been announced several times between 1856 and 1858 but had never been published. As the correspondence with his parents suggests, it might be possible that Verne was in financial disagreement with the director Pitre-Chevalier (1812-1863), who was not only a well-known journalist of his time, but also the distinguished author of historical works on Brittany. One of his publications, *Bretagne et Vendée: Histoire de la Révolution française dans l'ouest* (*Brittany and the Vendée: History of the French Revolution in the West*, 1845; reprinted in 1851 and 1859), might be among Verne's historical sources in writing *Chanteleine*. Pitre-Chevalier died suddenly on June 15, 1863, and was replaced by long-time colleague Charles Wallut (1829-1899). Wallut was among Verne's friends, even his "best friend" (as Verne wrote in a dedication of his book *De la Terre à la Lune* [*From the Earth to the Moon*], in 1865) and his collaborator for several plays written around 1860. So it is possible that Jules Verne resumed his work for *Musée des Familles* on Wallut's request. In December 1863 the magazine published Verne's short article on the balloon journey of his friend Nadar, "A propos du *Géant*" ("Concerning the *Giant*"), followed in April 1864 by the essay on Edgar Allan Poe and his works, preceding the printing of *The Count of Chanteleine* from October to December of the same year. In an— alas! undated—letter to Wallut, written from Paris, Verne announced: "Je suis en pleine Vendée. Cela me plaît beaucoup à faire." ("I am in the middle of the Vendée. It pleases me very much to write about it.")[3] Apart from the travel log, this is the only document we know of pertaining to the writing of *The Count of Chanteleine*.

---

3.   From the collection of Eric Weissenberg, as published in *Bulletin de la Société Jules Verne*, no. 140 (2001), 12-13.

ILLUSTRATIONS

One of the challenges in the Palik series is selecting illustrations, derived from the first French publication of Verne stories in the 19th century and the beginning of the 20th century. Most are either from the stories with which they appeared, or are from other Verne stories, choosing images to match the new context. In this volume, the engravings from *The Count of Chanteleine* are from the original French publication in magazine form, credited to Edmond Morin, A. de Bar and Foulquier, while those in the introduction are from other Verne novels.

The maps in the Notes section were created especially for this volume by **Garmt de Vries-Uiterweerd**.

We are particularly indebted to **Bernhard Krauth,** chairman of the German Jules-Verne-Club since 2005, for providing the illustrations from Verne stories. A deep sea licensed master working today as a docking pilot in Bremerhaven, Germany, Bernhard has published several Verne-related articles in France, the Netherlands and Germany. Intensely interested in the illustrations of the original French editions of Verne's work, he has been deeply involved in a project to digitize the illustrations, more than 5,000 in all. The project is for common, non-commercial use, and most of the illustrations in this publication were made possible through his generosity.

ACKNOWLEDGMENTS

The Palik series, spearheaded by the North American Jules Verne Society, represents a cooperative effort among Vernians worldwide, pooling the resources and knowledge of the various organizations in different countries. This particular volume represents a unique international collaboration, utilizing Verne experts from Canada, Germany, the Netherlands, and the United States. As work began, the North American Jules Verne Society learned that Verne experts in the Netherlands and the Czech Republic were finishing their own first translations of *Le Comte de Chanteleine* in their respective languages. This volume has benefitted from the input of Jan Rychlík and especially Garmt de Vries-Uiterweerd and the Jules Verne Genootschap, the Dutch Verne society. Further assistance has been rendered by internationally renowned Verne expert Volker Dehs. Their cooperation and expertise has much enriched this volume. It points to a future of collaboration between international Verne organizations, a trend that began in the 1990s with the creation of the Jules Verne listserv and website at jv.gilead.org.il by the late Zvi Har'El.

The Society is grateful for research assistance to Frédéric Jaccaud, curator of Jean-Michel Margot's Verne Collection at the Maison d'Ailleurs (House of Elsewhere) in Yverdon-les-Bains, Switzerland.

179

The Society also appreciates the efforts of members who have contributed to this volume, including Malcolm Henderson and Ross Bagby, and such friends as Elvira Berkowitsch, Jean Frodsham, Pachara Yongvongpaibul, and David March of the Rafael Sabatini website rafaelsabatini.com.

Peter Overstreet modified one of the orginal covers from the first French Hetzel editions of Jules Verne for this book. A professional Illustrator for two decades, he is director of "Legion Fantastique," the world's only Jules Verne re-enactment society.

Contributors

Edward Baxter is a graduate of Mount Allison University and the University of Toronto, and has also studied at the University of Lausanne. He taught French for nearly thirty years at Ontario secondary schools. From 1977 until retiring in 1986, Baxter was Head of Modern Languages at Don Mills Collegiate Institute in North York, where he was appointed for a one-year term in 1980 as the city's first Poet Laureate. Baxter has translated several hundred articles for the *Dictionary of Canadian Biography*, along with eight books. These include two distinguished new versions of Verne's *Family Without a Name* (1982) and *The Fur Country* (1987), both sponsored under the auspices of the Canada Council, published by the New Canada Press. After translating "The Humbug" for *The Jules Verne Encyclopedia* (Scarecrow Press, 1996), he contributed a series of new Verne translations for several publishers: *The Invasion of the Sea* (Wesleyan, 2001), *The Golden Volcano* (Nebraska, 2008), and the 1882 play *Journey Through the Impossible* (2003), copublished by Prometheus and the North American Jules Verne Society. Baxter contributed the first translation of "The Marriage of Mr. Anselme des Tilleuls" for the Society's book, *The Marriage of a Marquis*, along with "San Carlos" and *The Siege of Rome*, in the volume entitled *Bandits & Rebels*, all for the Palik Series.

Volker Dehs has studied modern philologies and arts at the universities of Göttingen (Germany) and Nantes (France). He translated into German five Verne novels and one short story, for which he also provided commentaries. He collaborated (with Olivier Dumas and Piero Gondolo della Riva) on the edition of the Verne-Hetzel Correspondance (Geneva, 5 volumes, 1999-2006). Dehs has found many forgotten Verne texts, such as plays, speeches, poems, and letters, which he published for the first time in French, mainly in the *Bulletin de la Société Jules Verne*. He wrote two Verne biographies in German in 1986 and 2005, which have been, respectively, translated into Spanish, and Turkish. He has authored some 150 articles on Verne, which have been published in French, German, English, Spanish, Portuguese, Dutch, Japanese and Polish. In 2002 he edited a bibliography of criticism on Verne in French and German, and is currently working on a comprehensive bibliography of Verne's works.

Brian Taves (Ph.D., University of Southern California) has been an archivist in the Motion Picture, Broadcasting, and Recorded Sound Division of the Library of Congress since 1990. He is the author of over 100 articles and 25 chapters in anthologies. Taves has also written books on P.G. Wodehouse and Hollywood; director Robert Florey; the genre of historical adventure movies; and fantasy-adventure writer Talbot Mundy, in addition to editing an original anthology of Mundy's best stories. In 2002-2003, Taves was chosen as Kluge Staff Fellow at the Library to write the first book on silent film pioneer Thomas Ince, to appear in 2011. Taves's writing on Verne has been translated into French, German, and Spanish, and he is currently writing a book on the 300 film and television adaptations of Verne worldwide. Taves is coauthor of *The Jules Verne Encyclopedia* (Scarecrow, 1996), and edited the first English-language publication of Verne's *Adventures of the Rat Family* (Oxford, 1993).

Garmt de Vries-Uiterweerd received his Ph.D. in physics from Utrecht University, the Netherlands, and currently works at Ghent University, Belgium. His field of research is astroparticle physics, the study of elementary particles of cosmic origin. He has been interested in Jules Verne since his early youth, creating one of the earliest websites dedicated to the French author. He has been an active member of the Dutch Jules Verne Society since its official formation in 1997, as webmaster, assistant editor of the society's magazine *De Verniaan*, and, since 2007, as president. De Vries-Uiterweerd has written numerous articles and chapters in books on Verne in Dutch as well as international publications. He edited the books *Jeugdherinneringen* (2008) and *In wrâldreis yn 80 dagen* (2010), the first ever Verne book in Frisian. De Vries-Uiterweerd has translated several of Jules Verne's texts to Dutch, with a focus on those texts that bring out little known aspects of Verne's work, such as *Les méridiens et le calendrier* (2005), *Souvenirs d'enfance et de jeunesse* (2008), and *Edgar Poe et ses œuvres* (2010). He has just finished the Dutch translation of *Le Comte de Chanteleine*, serialized in *De Verniaan* before being published as a volume.

THE PALIK SERIES

The last two decades have brought astonishing progress in the study of Jules Verne, with new translations of Verne stories, including the discovery of many texts. Still, there remain a number of his stories that have been overlooked, and it is this gap that the North American Jules Verne Society seeks to fill in the Palik series.

Through the generosity of our late member, Edward Palik, and the pooling of expertise by a variety of Verne scholars and translators around the world, we will be able to bring to the Anglophone public a series of hitherto unknown Verne tales.

Ed Palik had a special enthusiasm for bringing neglected Verne stories to English-speaking readers, and this will be reflected in the series that bears his name. In this way the society hopes to fulfill the goal that Ed's consideration has made possible. The volumes published will reveal the amazing range of Verne's storytelling, in genres that may surprise those who only know his most famous stories. We hope to allow a better appreciation of the famous writer who has, for more than a century and a half, been the widest-read author of fiction in the world.

www.ingramcontent.com/pod-product-compliance
Lightning Source LLC
Chambersburg PA
CBHW050402030726
47503CB00006B/1984